THE WHISPERS' ECHO

VALERIE KEOGH

First published in 2020 by Bloodhound Books.

www.bloodhoundbooks.com

Print ISBN 978-1-913419-80-6

ALSO BY VALERIE KEOGH

PSYCHOLOGICAL THRILLERS

The Three Women

The Perfect Life

THE DUBLIN MURDER MYSTERIES

No Simple Death

No Obvious Cause

No Past Forgiven

No Memory Lost

No Crime Forgotten (coming November 2020)

For my sisters, Heather and Deirdre.
With love.

Whispers
Soft hushed words
Often sweet
Sometimes vindictive
And venomous
Echoing
Over years
Their evil
Never fading.
Anon

1

It always started the same. Quiet, inoffensive whispers that tickled Melanie's ear and made the tiny hairs at the back of her neck stand on end. She would try to ignore the sound, hoping it would go away. But it never did and when she opened her eyes there would be a mouth close to her ear. Blood-red lips, tiny, startlingly-white teeth. Every time, she would shake off the sand of sleep, focus on the sibilant sound and try to make sense of what was being said.

'I can't hear you,' she'd plead. Every single time. 'Speak up.'

And the lips would grow bigger, cartoon-like, and the blood-red lipstick would leak into the miniscule creases that radiated from the mouth. But no matter how big they got, the whisper stayed eerily soft.

'I don't understand,' she'd cry, her voice loud and harsh.

The cartoon, clownish cupid's bow would vanish to be replaced by narrow lips contorted in anger.

'Please.'

The lips would twist, then open wide to expel foul air, and as Melanie recoiled, a louder sound would be driven out of the mouth from some deep hidden place of anguish. It would ricochet around the room, the volume rising until the deafening screech dragged an answering cry of torment from her and she would reach out with two trembling, pleading hands and beg over and over again to be told what the voice was trying to tell her.

The answer would come then, falling into the silence of the night, into the dream in which she tossed and turned as she tried to escape. Quietly said words that never lost their power, words that finally woke her, jerking her upright, the curdling stink of fear all around her as she listened to them echo around the room.

You're a murderer.

Every time, she hoped for a different answer, for the whole thing to have been a mistake, to wake and find that the reality was different, that all the bad things in her life were only there in her dreams.

And every time – every single time – she would sit with her hands pressed into the bed as the echo of the whispers grew fainter and sob for the one stupid mistake she had made, that one childish action she'd never managed to either forget or forgive herself for.

How could she?

She *was* a murderer.

2

Melanie Scott's fingers tightened on the empty wine glass she held as she let her gaze drift around the table. She couldn't help the surge of pride; she'd done it, despite everything, she was here in this pretty ghastly restaurant celebrating her amazing achievement... a junior partnership with Masters Corporate Law.

Although Blacks, a trendy London restaurant, was popular with Masters staff, she'd never been in it before. It was too overtly masculine for her taste; all dark wood and shiny brass fittings. Most of the clientele were employees from the surrounding finance and law offices, all of them trying too hard to look as if they were enjoying themselves even as their hard assessing eyes swept the room to see who else was there... who was celebrating... who looked to be drowning their sorrows.

The other junior partners, who had dragged her here to celebrate her promotion to their ranks, were quaffing bottles of expensive wine. As a rule, she didn't drink much and her head was buzzing from the few glasses she'd had. She'd asked the waiter for water, twice, but there was no sign of it coming. Looking around, she tried to catch his eye as he flitted past but instead caught the attention of a tall, handsome man leaning nonchalantly against the bar. A pint glass in one hand, he raised it towards her and smiled.

For a second that felt like an eternity, she locked eyes with him and then, embarrassed, she looked away. Moments later, she risked a quick look from the side of her eyes to find he was still staring in her direction. Her cheeks flushed with colour; she wasn't sure whether to be flattered or annoyed. It wasn't the kind of thing that normally happened to her. She gave a soft chuckle that was lost in the surrounding noise. It was the kind of thing that *never* happened to her. Maybe now that she was a partner, there would be more time for a little romance in her life. It had been way too long.

Her colleagues on both sides were deep in conversation and, from the snippets she overheard, business was being discussed. It was one of the reasons she tended to avoid these outings, the talk invariably circled around work and she spent enough time debating mergers and acquisitions during the course of the day without wanting to spend the evening doing the same. Especially tonight, an evening when she was supposed to be celebrating.

Picking up her bag, she murmured *the ladies* to no one in particular and slipped away, resisting the temptation to glance towards the bar to see if the man was still there, if he were watching. A smile curved her generous lips. How silly she was being. She was almost forty, not fourteen.

The ladies' room was, unusually, empty. It was also quiet and cool. She washed her hands and held them under the dryer as she stared into the mirror. Not bad, she supposed, tilting her head to check her hair. She'd pinned it into a tight chignon that morning and not a hair had dared go astray. It was a bit severe; she wondered about unpinning it and letting it fall loose around her shoulders. Her colleagues would be surprised at such a deviation from her usual corporate image; they might pass comment or think she was being flirtatious. No, she smoothed a hand over her head, she'd leave it as it was. With a step to the side, she checked her figure in the navy pencil skirt. She was a member of a gym but seldom had time to go, but as she rarely had time to eat either her weight was much as it had been when she was younger. Turning face-on again, she touched up her lipstick.

The man at the bar was incredibly handsome. Her silk shirt was buttoned to the neck. She reached up and opened the top three buttons, hastily buttoning up the lower one when the gap revealed the lacy edge of her bra... she wanted to look sexy not tarty. With a sigh, she fastened the next and met her pale-blue eyes in the mirror with a rueful smile. Honestly, one glance from a good-looking man and she was acting like an idiot. Her eyes softened. An idiot, maybe, but there had been something... a connection of sorts. She was certain she'd not imagined it. *Almost certain.*

Stepping back into the dimly-lit, noisy restaurant, she lifted her chin, took a deep breath and looked towards the bar, wishing she'd been brave enough to let her hair down, a toss of blonde locks would have been the perfect flirtatious come-on. But it would have been wasted. The man was gone. She almost laughed. What had she been thinking? He'd probably been looking across the room at someone else. Brushing aside a dart of disappointment, she chose instead to be amused at her silliness and headed towards the bar. 'A mineral water,' she said to the bartender, opening her bag to search for her purse.

'I'll get that,' a deep voice said, causing her to look up, then to drop her bag in confusion.

Typically, it landed upside down, dumping all the rubbish she kept inside in a pile on the floor. She bent to pick it up and so did he, but he was quicker, scooping the contents back inside and handing it to her with a grin that widened when he saw her flush of embarrassment. 'Nothing too naughty inside,' he said.

She wanted to say there was nothing at all naughty inside when she met his eyes. Warm brown with flecks of hazel, they softened as he smiled. He was teasing her, she realised, and she gave what she hoped was a flirtatious smile, not a grimace. This wasn't a game she was good at.

He turned to pay the bartender, then slid the glass of water along the bar towards her. 'Here you go.'

'Thank you.' She held the glass to her mouth and took a sip, taking another while she watched him. Up close, he was even better looking than she'd thought. Dark hair, ever so slightly too long so that it curled over the collar of his shirt, those amazing brown eyes and a firm mouth that looked as if it often smiled.

'Hugo Field,' he said, reaching out a hand to take hers.

He held it too long, his thumb caressing the back of her hand in slow sensuous circles. Melanie felt a frisson of lust hit her that seemed to numb her brain and make the rest of her body tingle. Blinking rapidly, she pulled her hand away. Okay, she needed to call a halt to this man's gallop. 'Melanie Scott.' She took another drink, hoping the cold water would reach parts that seemed to have suddenly overheated. 'Thank you for the water.' She kept her voice even with difficulty and nodded towards her table of colleagues. 'I'm with a group of people so I really should be getting back.'

He tilted his head a little and smiled. 'You sure? They don't look as if they're missing you, if you don't mind me saying. Why don't you stay here?'

Melanie drew herself up. 'No,' she said, firmly and unapologetically, her voice a little cooler. 'I need to return.'

He held a hand up quickly. 'Sorry, I didn't mean to push. It's...' He stared at her with those ridiculous brown eyes, eyes she could drown in. 'It's just that you look like someone I'd like to get to know.'

Feeling a flash of heat across her cheeks, she looked away. 'Unfortunately, it's my party,' she said, looking back to the table, knowing that if she didn't return, they'd not really notice, but it *was* her party and she wasn't going to leave early.

'A birthday?' When she shook her head, he reached out for her left hand, lifting it to stare at her ring finger, dropping it quickly before she'd a chance to complain. 'Not an engagement party, I'm pleased to see.'

Once again, his touch had electrified her, darts of heat shooting from her hand to parts she'd almost forgotten she had. 'It's a celebration,' she said, stumbling over her words, her tongue suddenly feeling too big for her mouth. She took another drink. 'I've recently made junior partner in the firm I work for.'

'You're an accountant?'

She shook her head, wishing once again she'd been brave enough to let her hair down. 'A lawyer, a corporate lawyer to be exact.' She hadn't needed to be specific, but she wanted him to be impressed. Corporate lawyers were an elite group, top of the pecking order. Melanie Scott, she wanted him to know, to be quite clear about, wasn't a woman to be messed with.

He lifted his drink and smiled. 'Well then, Melanie Scott, corporate lawyer, newly-minted junior partner, if you won't stay with me now, how about meeting me for dinner some night?'

Wasn't this all a little unbelievable? What was that trite expression – *if something looks too good to be true, it usually is.* She looked around the busy restaurant, a slight frown appearing between her eyes, suspicion lurking in her next words. 'You were here on your own?'

'No, I too was with some colleagues. They left to return home to their wives. I was finishing my drink and was about to leave when I looked across the room and saw you. Staying to watch you seemed infinitely preferable to returning to my empty apartment.' He laughed then, a contagious sound that brought an answering smile to her lips. 'Bloody hell, I sound like a right sad weirdo.'

'No,' she said, liking his honesty. 'You sound nice.' She reached into her bag, unzipped a pocket and took out a business card. 'My email address. I'm in and out of so many meetings, it's impossible to have my phone switched on. I always check my emails though, so it's the easiest way to contact me.' It wasn't the truth. She simply didn't like giving out her phone number to people she didn't know, no matter how incredibly attractive they were.

With a final smile, she thanked him again for the water and headed back to her colleagues, feeling his eyes following her, resisting the temptation to look back. She doubted if anyone at the table had noticed she'd gone. Or maybe one person, she realised, catching a woman's eye across the table. Jane Robinson, the only other female partner.

Jane had been the first to congratulate Melanie on her promotion. 'Another female to dilute the testosterone-charged meetings will make my life so much easier,' she'd said. That might very well be, but Melanie had noticed Jane chose to sit the other side of the table from her rather than beside her. Obviously, she wanted the testosterone diluted, not removed.

Jane's amused look and raised eyebrow told her she'd seen the encounter at the bar. Melanie gave a careless shrug but felt a level of satisfaction. Maybe Jane would see there was more to her than the quiet woman who beavered away in her office.

It was another hour before the party finally broke up. Melanie, who had watched Hugo leave with a twinge of regret, was bored by the end and wanted to go home. Luckily, they all insisted that as guest of honour she could have the first taxi.

With a fixed smile, she thanked everyone for their good wishes and climbed in, the smile fading as soon as it pulled away. She slumped back and shut her eyes, feeling herself drift off as the taxi negotiated London streets and traffic, then it stopped and she was outside her apartment in Fulham.

'Can you wait until I'm inside?' she asked, adding a generous tip when the driver grunted a *yes*. Gathering her belongings, she climbed out, realising too late that it had started to rain, big cold drops peppering her blouse as she made a run for the door. With a wave of thanks to the driver, she turned the key and stepped inside, feeling the warmth hit her with a sigh of pleasure.

The two-bedroomed apartment she called home was the ground floor of an Edwardian house. The upper apartment, with its front door down a side passage, was owned by a businessman who spent most of the year in Hong Kong. Melanie had met him only once in the three years she'd lived there. She'd liked the apartment as soon as she had viewed it and when she'd stood in the spacious lounge, and the estate agent had opened the French windows into the small private garden where espaliered fruit trees covered every wall, she knew she had to have it. Luckily, the rest of the apartment was perfect; a small kitchen, a well-appointed bathroom and two good-sized bedrooms. It had stretched her budget to the maximum but it was an oasis of calm in what was often her crazily exhausting world and she'd never regretted it.

Heading straight to her bedroom, she undressed, hanging her suit up and throwing her blouse and underwear into the laundry basket. She half-heartedly removed her make-up and minutes later was crawling between the sheets. Almost asleep, her eyes snapped open on a gasp when she heard a ping from her mobile alerting her to the arrival of an email. Normally, she'd have set it to *do not disturb* but she'd forgotten, or maybe she'd hoped Hugo would contact her. It had to be him. Who else would send one so late?

Stretching out, she fumbled for the lamp switch and grabbed her phone. A shiver of excitement rushed through her, making her feel like a teenager. It was him! A short email. *Hi Melanie, I can't wait to see you again. Dinner? Tomorrow night?*

She'd a vague idea she should be playing hard to get or something, that he shouldn't assume that she was available on a Saturday night but, he liked her, she certainly liked him, what was the point? Wasn't that the best thing about *not* being a teenager, you didn't have to play silly games. She tapped out, *Yes. Sounds perfect*. Then, afraid he might suggest picking her up and she wasn't stupid enough to give her address to a virtual stranger, she added, *I'll meet you in the same place at eight.*

Seconds later, as she sat fighting sleep, another ping told her he'd replied. *Perfect, see you then.*

She switched off the light and lay back. Well, well, what a wonderful end to a wonderful day. On a sigh of pleasure, she shut her eyes and drifted off on a wave of unusual contentment.

She wasn't sure how long she'd been asleep when she heard the ping again, opening her eyes and looking towards where her phone sat. Hugo again? A frisson of pleasure ran through her, a girlish excitement she hadn't felt in a long time. With an expectant smile, she switched on the light again and reached for the phone.

The smile faded when she saw the sender wasn't Hugo as she'd expected. She shuffled closer to the circle of light thrown by the lamp, held the phone up and squinted to read, *nobody@gmail.com*. How very odd.

She should have ignored it or left it until the morning, but curiosity made her open it, her eyes widening when she read what was written – a name that made her gasp and drop the phone. With startled eyes, she looked at it for a moment, unable to move, afraid to pick it up again. She gave a short unconvincing laugh. It had been a stressful few weeks and an exhausting day; she'd fallen asleep and had a bad dream. That's all it was. A dream or rather, she amended, thinking of the name she thought she'd seen, a nightmare.

The phone was lying face down on the duvet. She reached for it, flipping it over as fear gripped her insides. A low keening sound of despair pushed its way through gritted teeth as she read the words on the screen and she jumped from the bed, the phone flying to land with a dull thump on the carpet. She watched it as she stood naked and shivering, half-expecting it to move as if possessed like an escapee from a Stephen King novel. She held a hand over her mouth and concentrated on breathing slowly, trying to calm down. It had to be wrong, a trick of the light.

She stepped closer to the phone but the email had closed. It took a few seconds to gather the courage to bend, pick it up and turn it on. But it wasn't a trick of the light, or a very bad dream. There, clear as day, a name she'd hoped never to see again. A name that reminded her that leaving her past behind didn't mean she was ever going to escape it.

Anne Edwards.

3

Throwing the phone onto the bed, Melanie backed away from it. Fear made her jittery, her eyes flitting from side to side, looking for escape or at least a safe place. With a final glance at the phone she hurried across to the spare bedroom and shut the door behind her, leaning her weight against it as if afraid something would try to follow. But it already had, hadn't it? *Someone knew.* Someone knew and wanted her to know they knew. They didn't have to spell out the consequences; everything she'd worked so hard for would be destroyed if the truth about her past got out.

She shut her eyes on the thought, opening them quickly when she saw her mother's face, the hard eyes and the embittered screwed-up mouth waiting as always, to criticise. *You've made a mess of it. You'll never change.* Melanie could hear the cutting words now as she'd heard them so many times growing up, the background music not only to her failures, rare as they were, but to the successes too. The honours exam results, the prizes, the first at university, all were accompanied by her mother's sour dismissive, *All very well but it won't last, you'll make a mess of it again, you always do.*

As Melanie's world spun out of control, the floor swayed under her feet. She made it to the bed before the stars that appeared around the edge of her vision winked out. It would have been better to stay there deep in the retreat of oblivion, to hide away from pain, fear, and her mother's scathing, cutting voice. She would have done so, but hours later the chill of her naked body woke her.

She reached for the duvet that lay folded neatly across the end of the unmade bed and pulled it over her, covering her head, seeking heat and comfort, desperate to return to that unconscious state where she didn't have to think. Exhausted, she fell into a restless sleep.

It didn't last. She woke again feeling groggy, looking around the spare bedroom with a puzzled frown before it all came back to her and she shut her eyes tightly and gulped.

Anne Edwards.

Melanie never thought to see or hear that name again. With a growl of frustration, she threw the duvet off, swung her feet to the floor and stood, pushing her tangled hair back with an unsteady hand. The vague hope that it had all been some ridiculously crazy nightmare took her to her own bedroom where she stood and glared at her phone as if it were to blame for everything. Holding her breath, she reached for it and tapped the email icon. Her breath was released on a hiss of agitation. The email hadn't changed, the sender still *nobody@gmail.com.* Her fingers itched to tap out a reply, to demand to know who this was, what they knew. Instead, she dropped it on the bed. Who it was, and what they knew would be helpful, but really what she wanted to know was why?

Anne Edwards. That was almost twenty-five years ago.

Picking up her phone again, Melanie checked the time and swore. She was supposed to be meeting a friend at one and it was twelve thirty. Scrolling through her contacts, she found Caitlin's number and rang it.

'I'm so sorry,' Melanie said, when it was answered, 'I'm not going to be able to make lunch.' She barely heard the reply as she worried over the email and it was only when she heard Caitlin call her name on a note of irritation that Melanie realised she'd zoned out. She pulled herself back into the conversation. 'Sorry, Caitlin, I missed what you said.'

'I said I was so looking forward to hearing all about your promotion and the celebration dinner.'

'And I'll tell you, I promise, only not today. I barely slept and I'm shattered. I'll be in touch soon and we can meet up for a glass of wine. And...' Melanie added, knowing it was something her friend would be more than interested to hear, 'believe it or not, I met someone last night.' She hung up on a squeal of *tell me more* and sat unmoving for a long time before getting up, having a shower and dressing in comfy stretch trousers and a sweatshirt.

With the phone clasped in her hand, she made coffee, took it into the living room and sank into the chair near the French windows. This was her place of relaxation; she'd stare out across the small but perfect garden and watch the changing colours of the seasons in the trees and shrubs and feel more in tune with the world. It was a beautiful, magical place and, normally, it worked its power on her. But not today. She stared blankly, her fingers wrapped around the mug of coffee so tightly that they ached, her back rigid and tense, head spinning.

It wasn't until the coffee was gone that she picked up the phone again to check her emails. Not the one from *nobody* this time but the ones from Hugo. A quiver of sadness fluttered through her that the excitement of meeting him had been spoilt by dirty fingers reaching from her past. Her mother's unforgiving voice buzzed in Melanie's ear, and despair swept through her, fogging her brain, making rational thought impossible.

With the hope that more caffeine might help clear her head, she made another mug and with it cupped between her hands, she took sips and tried to think of who might have sent that email.

There were a few possibilities, of course, people she'd known back then. She tapped her nails on the side of the mug, beating out a reflective tattoo. But why now, after all these years? *Anne Edwards.* The sadness of regret was a weight in Melanie's chest that had never really gone away. She sighed, loud and long, the sound floating on the air before fading and taking with it any hopes she had for her meeting with Hugo that night. There was no point. He'd probably felt sorry for her, the clumsy woman who'd dropped her bag. What on earth would a charming, handsome, very attractive man see in her? She wondered if she should strike first, email and say she had to cancel. She growled in frustration and pushed her fingers through her hair. Didn't she deserve a bit of happiness? *Anne Edwards.* That was a different time, Melanie had been a different person. Hot tears of self-pity welled and trickled. Would she never be through with paying for what she'd done?

Brushing the tears away, she wrote an email to Hugo to cancel dinner, explaining that something had come up. Her finger hovered over the arrow to send it but she couldn't bring herself to take that final step and threw the phone down with it unsent. For the rest of the afternoon, it went around and around, the belief that she'd never atone for what she'd done vying with a desperate desire for happiness. She was already tired, and the dilemma exhausted her.

By five, still undecided, she was sitting, aimlessly staring out at the garden when she was startled by a loud ping. Another email. She looked at the phone warily and felt a belt of tension tighten around her forehead. Her hand slid across the small table to pick up the phone, then with a quick indrawn breath, she pressed the key. It was from Hugo. *Looking forward to seeing you tonight.* Her breath released on a sigh as a shiver of anticipation swept through her. It was followed by the first stirring of anger. She wanted this; she wasn't going to listen to her mother's poisonous whispers anymore nor was she going to let a stupid email dictate how she was going to live her life.

She spent the next twenty minutes choosing what to wear. When she spent as long picking out the right underwear, she refused to acknowledge the little voice reminding her that sleeping with a man on a first date was not her style. Maybe it was time to change that. She smoothed a hand over the fitted silver-grey dress. She was a mature woman, what was she waiting for? In her experience, men like Hugo Field didn't appear too often.

It took determination but she put the other email out of her mind and headed out as the taxi she'd ordered arrived. She tried to relax as the driver made the usual small talk, answering automatically as nervous anticipation made her shift restlessly in her seat. Outside Blacks, she paid the fare, got out and took a few steps towards the restaurant, then turned and took a step backwards towards the idling taxi. It was a bad idea, she'd go home. Just as this thought was solidifying, the restaurant door opened and Hugo came striding out, hand extended, smiling warmly.

When she put her hand into his, he pulled her close and planted a kiss on one cheek then the other. It was a common greeting and didn't mean anything more than *hello* so why did she feel as if it was the first movement in a complicated dance, the steps of which she wasn't sure she knew. She wanted to appear sophisticated and chic, she felt gauche and clumsy, afraid to speak in case the words that came out let her down.

He smiled at her. 'You look lovely,' he said, very much in

control of the situation, his eyes sweeping over her, lingering on her mouth. 'I wasn't sure what kind of food you liked but there's a little Italian restaurant a short walk away if you'd be happy with that.'

'Perfect,' she said, relieved he didn't want to eat in Blacks. She was feeling stupidly overwhelmed by him and his obvious admiration; a walk in the fresh air might be what she needed to cool down. 'I love Italian,' she added, falling into step beside him.

They brushed against each other as they walked but she was pleased he didn't reach for her hand and at the same time a little disappointed. Aware she was behaving like an immature schoolgirl, she reminded herself that she was a partner in a prestigious law firm. An intelligent woman, not one given to going all weak at the knees when a handsome man paid her a bit of attention. She had to bite her lip on the giggle that wanted to escape because like it or not, her knees felt decidedly wobbly.

The restaurant was, as he'd promised, only a five-minute walk. He did most of the talking on the way, telling her of an art exhibition he'd been to earlier. Art wasn't something that interested her, and talk of technique and artists whose names she'd never heard of went over her head. But she was mesmerised by the sound of his voice, the way he used his hands as he spoke and the enthusiasm and energy he seemed to radiate.

She'd never been comfortable talking about herself and would have been quite happy if he'd continued to dominate the conversation, but over dinner, after a couple of glasses of wine, she found herself relaxing and becoming expansive as she answered his questions, talking about the excitement of her very recent promotion, her hopes to have more high-profile and challenging clients and her work in general.

He seemed sincerely interested, asked her intelligent questions and she found herself opening up more than normal. She stopped on an embarrassed laugh. 'Now you know all about me, or at least about what I do, so it's your turn.'

He lifted his glass, swirled the wine and took a sip. 'I'm an architect.'

An architect. She was impressed; perhaps that explained his interest in art, didn't they have to be artistic as well as practical? She searched for something knowledgeable to ask, came up blank and settled for asking, 'Have you designed anything I might have seen?'

He laughed. 'I wish. No, I mainly work on private commissions. I find it suits me better than working for a big corporation. It does take me away a lot though, which is the downside, especially...' He reached for her hand and held it. 'Especially if there is someone I'm interested in seeing again.'

She could feel the heat from his fingers sear her skin. For a few seconds she found it difficult to breathe, then he took his hand away and she felt bereft. 'Where...' She stopped as the word came out as a squeak. With an apologetic smile she picked up her water glass and took a mouthful. 'Sorry. The air is quite dry in here. Where do you work?'

'Mostly on the continent. My most recent commissions have been in Slovakia and Russia.'

'Wow, that must be fascinating,' she said, when what she really wanted to ask was how often he was away, how long for, and when was he away next.

'Yes,' he admitted. 'Fascinating and challenging.' He pushed his empty wine glass away. 'Would you like something else?' He waited until she shook her head before holding up a hand for the waiter.

'We should split it,' Melanie said when the bill arrived.

He was looking at it, his eyes flicked up to catch hers. 'If you remember, I asked you to dinner,' he said. 'When you invite me, you can pay.'

It seemed fair to her and it also gave her the perfect opening to suggest meeting again. 'I had a lovely evening,' she said. Then, the words tripping over themselves in their haste to be said, added, 'I'd love to do it again and I know a very nice Spanish restaurant I could take you to.' She waited, her breathing on hold, as he took cash from his wallet for the bill.

'Spanish? Sounds interesting, I'd like that,' he said, putting the money on the silver tray.

Her exhale was soft, satisfied, tinged with excitement. 'Excellent. When would suit you?' She wanted him to say tomorrow, hoped he would, her initial pleasure dimming as he appeared to give her question more thought than she deemed necessary, trying to keep her smile from wavering when he gave his considered answer.

'How about next Friday?'

Swallowing her disappointment, she nodded as if that were her preferred day too. 'Friday suits me perfectly.'

Out on the street, more disillusionment awaited. She thought he'd suggest going somewhere else for a drink, maybe even drop a hint about going back to her apartment but instead he raised his hand to hail a passing taxi.

'That was lucky,' he said, looking back to her. 'I'll email you during the week and we can firm up arrangements for Friday. Thank you for a very enjoyable evening.' When the taxi drew up alongside, he bent and kissed her on both cheeks again, then opened the door. Any thought that he was coming with her was quickly dispelled as he closed the door firmly and gave her a casual wave.

She gave the driver her address and sat back, feeling confused and a little numb. Had she misread all the signals? They'd been there, hadn't they? Shaking her head, she heaved a sad sigh of regret but by the time the taxi pulled up outside her apartment, she was starting to see the funny side of it all and gave a chuckle to think of the time she'd spent choosing sexy lingerie. Amusement was quickly followed by embarrassed annoyance at her childish excitement at his attention, her almost pathetic fawning over him. He was probably married or had a girlfriend in every country he worked in. She'd had a lucky escape she told herself as she climbed from the taxi. But when she opened the door into her quiet, elegant apartment where normally she felt a sense of peace, that night she felt the nagging pang of loneliness.

She'd blamed her job all these years for her single state and, in truth, the long hours didn't lend themselves to relationships, but other people did it. Her colleague, Jane, for instance, had been married for years. Throwing her coat on a kitchen chair, Melanie filled the kettle, switched it on and stood leaning back against the counter trying to rid herself of the feeling of rejection and the sour taste of disappointment. There had been lovers over the years, of course, but nobody who'd lasted more than a few months and nobody whose departure left her saddened. Maybe, she was one of those women who was destined to remain single.

The click of the kettle broke into her thoughts and automatically she reached for camomile tea. She left the bag in the mug to infuse and took it to the living room where she opened the French windows and stepped outside. It was a cold night but the high walls that surrounded the garden gave it a microclimate of its own and only in the depths of winter was it too cold to sit out. Earlier showers had been heavy, branches were still dripping and there was the scent of wet greenery and soil hanging in the air.

Tipping water from a garden chair, she sat and let out a long defeated sigh. The evening still puzzled her. The outcome so far removed from what she'd expected, from the signals he'd given. Had she done something to put him off? Said something wrong?

Melanie felt her eyes fill. She was being stupid. Even if her expectations had been met and she'd spent the night with Hugo, nothing would have come of it. Nothing *could* have. The shadow of Anne Edwards would have fallen over it and in the chill of that shadow, it would have withered and died.

Anne Edwards. Melanie looked back into the living room to where she'd dropped her bag on the sofa. She pulled the teabag from her mug, chucked it into the shrubbery and took a sip; but camomile tea didn't have sufficient soothing properties to make up for the tension that tightened around her forehead as her eyes lingered on her bag. Finally, with a soft growl, she put her mug down on a flagstone and headed inside.

She'd only taken a small clutch bag with her to the restaurant and when she opened it her brightly-coloured phone stood out, almost taunting her. It wasn't until she was sitting back on the garden chair that she looked at it, relief coming in a whoosh of exhaled breath to see that there were no more emails from *nobody*. There was, however, one from Hugo. She couldn't help the jolt of pleasure in seeing it nor the pathetically grateful sigh as she read, *You made me feel like a teenager tonight, I wanted so much to kiss you but I was afraid if I did, that I'd never want to let you go. Rushing you into a taxi seemed to be the safest thing to do. Friday can't come soon enough.*

She wanted to cheer, to whoop in relief that she hadn't somehow made a mess of it and then shook her head, feeling stupid for being so elated. But she was still smiling when she finished her tea, locked the doors, and headed to bed.

Her good mood lasted until an unsettling thought crossed her mind. Someone knew about Anne Edwards. Would they have gone to the trouble of setting up an email address simply to send her that one message? It was unlikely. Very unlikely.

The unsettling thought turned into a shiver of despair as, with grim certainty, she knew there was more to come.

4

Sunday was normally Melanie's day to relax, catch up with housework, do some grocery shopping.

She kept busy, and if her thoughts drifted she guided them firmly towards Hugo. Finally, she sat on the sofa with her dinner on a tray and tried to find something entertaining on TV, giving up in the end and picking up the book she'd been reading. She'd read a few chapters when she heard the ping that dragged her reluctantly back from the story to her apartment, her eyes widening as they slid to her phone. Tension ratcheted up immediately, and she felt her insides cramp. It could be Hugo, of course, but she knew it wasn't.

Swinging her feet to the floor, she stretched out and grabbed her phone. Her instincts had been correct, it was *nobody* and the message was the same. *Anne Edwards.* Nothing more.

Again, she was tempted to send a reply, her fingers hovering over the keys. What would she say? What could she say except *why* or *who*? With a grunt of frustration, she dropped the phone onto the sofa beside her and relaxed against the cushions, her thoughts slipping back through the years to the pretty, naïve fifteen-year-old, Anne. One of the counsellors she'd seen over the years, and there'd been many, had said she needed to forgive herself for what she'd done because until she did so, the pain of guilt would continue to eat away. But, of course, she hadn't been able to tell them the whole truth, making a vague reference to something regrettable in her youth. They hadn't pushed her for more, maybe seeing the set look that came on her face whenever she thought about what she'd done.

Only one counsellor had been bluntly honest. Crossing stubby arms across a flat chest, she'd looked directly at Melanie. 'I don't know why you wanted to see me if you've no intention of telling the truth. You're wasting your time and money. If you were looking for a magic get-out-of-jail card, let me tell you, it doesn't exist.'

Melanie had smiled, appreciating the honesty, but if the counsellor had thought it would be the wake-up call that she needed, she'd been wrong. Melanie had stood, thanked her and left, and she'd never seen a counsellor again. It meant that the guilty pain lingered and sometimes it overwhelmed her but, mostly, she'd learned to live with it.

When it overwhelmed her, like tonight, it proved itself a poor bed-companion. The dream that had haunted her since her childhood returned, as it often did, to leave her shaken. When she finally got back to sleep the remainder of the night was a series of restless periods of slumber filled with dark shadows and creeping menace interrupted by wide-awake moments where memories reeled and spun. She gave up when her clock hit five, climbing wearily from bed and standing for a long time under a cool shower, hoping it would make a difference. If it did, it wasn't obvious when she looked in the mirror.

With careful application of slightly more make-up than usual, she looked a little better and satisfied, she headed to work at the same time as she'd done since she'd started with Masters Corporate Law. As junior partner, she didn't need to be in the office quite as early but habits of a lifetime were hard to break. Anyway, she'd been told her office was ready and being in the newly-painted, small but quite swish office beat sitting at home wondering what was going to happen next. That something was going to happen, she was sure of. Whoever *nobody* was, they weren't going to be content with letting her know they knew, they'd do something more, or perhaps ask for something. *Blackmail*. It had been in the back of her mind since she'd first seen the email. It would, she thought, account for why whoever it was had waited this long. As a partner, even a junior one, she was set to make seriously good money. Someone wanted their share, to make her pay for what she'd done all those years before.

Her new office was on the second floor. It was small and simply furnished with a desk, two chairs, a tall filing cabinet and a strangely ornate coat hook on the back of the door. A square bay window overlooking the street to the front of the building provided maximum light. Through the side panels of glass on the left of the bay, she could see the front door and watch the coming and going of staff, briefcases either clasped under their arms or swinging casually from their hands. A great place to people-watch if she had the time.

She'd been invited to her first meeting with the senior partners at ten; she had time to spare but things she could be doing rather than staring out the window. There were a few personal belongings remaining in her old shared office, she collected them, put them away and looked around the room with a sense of pride. Here she'd continue the work she loved, the intricacies of mergers and acquisitions, the complexities of due-diligence reports and the simple, but necessary, background checks that were part and parcel of her job. She swung around in her chair to look at the window again. It needed a plant; she'd get one at the weekend.

With everything sorted, she switched on her computer and

checked for any new reports or emails. There were a couple of each, easily and quickly dealt with and she was about to switch off when she saw there were still twenty minutes remaining before the meeting. Almost of their own volition, her fingers flew over the keyboard and typed the name Hugo Field into the search area.

She'd thought about doing it the day before but, although she knew people did it all the time, she'd resisted, almost nervous about checking him out, afraid she'd find out he was married or wasn't who he said he was. Her friend, Caitlin, said she never went on a date without doing a thorough background check first. 'It's simply a new tool in an old battle,' she'd said when Melanie had raised an eyebrow. Now, here she was with Hugo's name in the search field, about to do what she'd silently criticised her friend for doing. With only a slight hesitation, she pressed the return key.

It was, to her surprise, a common name. She discounted the first few; the estate agent, jazz musician and the gardener, scrolling down, her eyes peering at the information and flicking to the time on the corner of the screen. Still ten minutes to spare but there were several pages to scroll through. It was on the third page that she found him, eyes narrowing to peer at the thumbnail photo at the top of the screen above the beautifully calligraphed *Hugo Field, Architect*. There was no mistake. It was a simple website detailing his qualifications, showing photographs of finished commissions and inviting people to contact him for terms and conditions. No personal details at all which was a little disappointing but not, she supposed, unexpected.

She stared at his photo, feeling her pulse race a little. He was so handsome, and even in this small business photo she could see his eyes were kind. With an eye on the time, she took a screenshot, edited out the text and sent the photo to her phone.

It was time to go. She switched off the computer, slipped on her jacket and checked herself in the small mirror she kept in the drawer of her desk. Not a hair out of place and, apart from the hint of sadness she saw lurking in her eyes that even looking at Hugo's photo hadn't managed to dispel, she looked fine. She fixed her expression into one suitable for a corporate lawyer and hurried from the office.

The structure within Masters followed what they liked to refer to as tradition even though the company had been formed a mere twenty years before. There were three senior partners, ten junior partners, and senior and junior associates whose numbers were dynamic, mainly because many quickly discovered that the generous salaries came with long hours and the high expectation that Masters came before everything else.

Moving up the ranks was a slow process as people rarely left Masters of their own accord. Six weeks earlier, when one of the senior partners passed away following a short illness, the shocked silence that followed his death was quickly filled with speculative muttering as to who would be promoted from the junior partner ranks, and in turn who would be promoted to junior partner from among the senior associates.

Melanie wasn't the longest-serving senior associate but she had worked hard over the years, always first in the office in the morning and last to leave at night. She was also diligent and uncomplaining and if there were envious eyes turned her way when she was promoted, the same people acknowledged the decision was a good one.

It *had* been a good one, Melanie was excellent at what she did. Meeting Hugo was the cherry on top of it all. She tried to push the thoughts of *nobody* from her mind as she waited for the lift to take her to the top floor where the senior partners had offices.

It was also where the conference room was situated and it

was here that the meeting was to be held. Melanie hesitated in the corridor outside before she went in, nervously smoothing a hand over her hair, straightening the sleeve of the jacket, adjusting the collar of her shirt. It wasn't a large room and it was dominated by a square mahogany table with a matching, incredibly uncomfortable-looking chair at each side. The fours chairs were identical but she knew if she sat it would be in the wrong one, so she stayed standing, moving over to the small window to stare out at the puffs of cloud that skittered by in the bright blue winter sky.

Her fingers tightened on the windowsill. This should be her moment, payback for the years of hard work she'd put in, a chance to move on and put her past well and truly behind her. She should be feeling pride and satisfaction but, instead, her head echoed with that name from her past.

She pushed it away and focused on memories of Hugo's amazing brown eyes. It was surprisingly effective and she was in a calmer frame of mind when the partners arrived five minutes after the hour. They strode in, their jackets left behind in their offices, shirtsleeves rolled up, ties loosened, but she wasn't fooled by their artfully casual appearance. These men, she knew, had balls of steel.

Within seconds, she was sorry she'd put her jacket on. The room was warm and the sun, low in the sky, was slanting her way. Even worse, the seat she was directed to was only several inches from a tall, modern radiator that was pumping out heat. Trying not to let her discomfort show, she sat with both feet on the ground and her hands resting one on top of the other on the table in front of her as she waited to hear what they had to say.

Richard Masters, son of the founder William Masters and as such considered the more senior of the senior partners, sat in the middle position. He was a thin man with stylishly-cut thick white hair and a remarkably deep voice. Melanie had always found him intimidating. 'We'd like to offer you our congratulations on your promotion. You've impressed us all' – he inclined his head towards each of his colleagues – 'with your dedication, commitment and attention to detail.' Clearing his throat, he reached for his water glass and took a sip before continuing. 'We're not the only ones either. You did some work for Fanton's Investment Management last year and they were so impressed that they've asked for you, personally, to handle their upcoming merger with CityEast Investment.' He stopped to allow this news to sink in.

Stunned, Melanie felt excitement bubble. She'd expected to be given more high-profile clients but this exceeded everything. These were two well-regarded investment institutions. 'That's excellent news,' she said, trying to keep her voice professionally neutral. 'I'm honoured to be offered such high-profile clients and I assure you I will give them one hundred per cent.'

Richard smiled slightly as if one hundred per cent was the least they'd expect. 'I'll have all the necessary information sent to you, and of course you may co-opt as many associates as you think you'll need.'

She'd need a couple, at least; there was going to be mountains of documentation to check, negotiations to manage, reports to complete. The rest of the meeting went by in a blur. When she realised the room had fallen silent around her, she dragged herself back, looked from expectant face to expectant face and wondered what it was she'd been asked. 'Sorry…?'

'I merely commented that it was a shame your mother couldn't be here to see your success,' Richard said patiently.

Her mother. Melanie pressed her lips together and looked down to shield her lying eyes, hoping he'd see her reaction as sorrow. When her mother had died, several years before, she'd taken the opportunity to reinvent their relationship, mentioning to colleagues how supportive her mother had been over the years, making her past sound happy and normal. Melanie had told the same lie when she'd been promoted to senior associate, telling the senior partners then how proud her mother would have been, the lie almost sticking in her throat because she knew her mother would have said exactly what she'd said at every single success, big and small, a variation on the same belittling, soul-destroying words she always used.

'Yes,' she said now, looking at him. 'She would have been very proud.'

'If that's all?' Richard said, with a glance at his colleagues who both inclined their heads in agreement.

'Before I go,' she said, quickly, 'I'd like to take this opportunity to thank you all for your faith in me, I promise you I will do everything in my power to ensure it is warranted.'

'I have no doubt,' Richard said with an enigmatic smile.

And that was it. She stood and made her exit, her head buzzing with excitement. On the second floor, she passed her office and continued along the corridor to the staffroom, grateful to find it empty. She took off her jacket and opened the small window that looked out onto the side wall of another building only a few feet away. A slight breeze carrying the scent of spices from the Indian restaurant next door drifted in. Cool and aromatic, it chilled her body and calmed her mind. This merger was exactly what she needed. Making plans and devising strategies were her forte. It was what made her the perfect corporate lawyer.

Taking a coffee back to her office, she sat and switched on her laptop to find that Richard had already sent the relevant details of the proposed merger and over the next few hours she read through them, taking copious notes and scribbling ideas as she went. It was going to be all-consuming, she decided when she finished. Luckily, her other cases were almost finished, merely requiring a few formalities before completion.

By the time she decided to finish for the day, she'd organised several meetings, chosen a couple of associates who weren't bogged down in their own cases to give her a hand and had drawn up a plan of what needed to be done.

It wasn't until she'd opened the door into her apartment later than usual that evening that she realised she hadn't given either Hugo or *nobody* a thought since early morning. She suspected she'd blown both up out of proportion. For goodness' sake, she'd only met Hugo once and she'd turned him into a knight in shining armour and as for those silly emails, a quiver ran through her as she attempted a brave, dismissive, 'Pshaw'. She'd forget about them, this merger needed her undivided attention, there was no room for romantic nonsense or worrying about her past. Fixing herself some dinner, she sat at the kitchen table to eat, half watching the news, half thinking about her day. The senior partners had put a lot of trust in her, she was determined not to let them down.

She rarely drank during the week but she felt a celebration was in order. There was a bottle of Chablis in the fridge; she opened it, poured a small glass and took it through to the living room. It would have been pleasant to sit outside but heavy rain pattering against the glass told her that wasn't to be. Instead, leaving the lights out, she pulled a small sofa nearer to the French window and sat with her glass of wine listening to the almost hypnotic sound of the raindrops.

It wasn't her wine glass falling to the carpeted floor that woke her, gasping from a dream where something was trying to grab her, blocking her path no matter which way she ran, something with long feelers and gaping drooling suckers. It had been a scarily creepy dream but it wasn't the reason her eyes snapped open. It had been a noise. Fear swept over her in a wave and she stood, moving away from the windows, her eyes searching the room. Was there somebody here? But there was enough light drifting in from the hallway to show her that she was alone. Holding her breath, she listened but if there was someone in the apartment, they were being as quiet as she. It took a few seconds for the truth to hit her and she dropped onto the sofa behind her. Of course there was nobody in the apartment. Her dream had momentarily disorientated her. The sound that had woken her, she knew what it was now, her mobile alerting her to a new email.

Knowledge of what had woken her didn't wipe away the fear; her heart was racing, an acrid smell of terror drifting up from the open neck of her shirt. Her phone was on the hall table. With slow steps, she went out and picked it up. She knew with a terrifying certainty who it was and what it would say.

She was only half right.

5

Melanie opened the email and read the message. She was so sure she would see *Anne Edwards* that she was confused when she didn't. Her eyes flicked back to the sender. Yes, it was from *nobody*. But instead of the name she'd expected to see, there were two words. *It's time.*

Fear was a strange emotion; she'd experienced it in a variety of ways over the years but it was always defined by something more understandable – the fear of being found out, of failure, of losing, of people knowing her secret, of her mother's cutting words – but this gut-wrenching fear was something different. *It's time.* For what? To pay for what she had done all those years ago? Was that what this was all about? Someone had found out about her past and wanted payment to keep quiet. Simple blackmail? Perhaps it was time to ask. Moving into the kitchen, she sat at the table and stared at the screen. She took a deep steadying breath and before she could change her mind, tapped out a two-word question, *What for*?

She waited, staring at the screen till her eyes became dry, blinking quickly as if she were afraid to miss the reply. But her phone stayed obstinately silent. Exhaustion and a deep sense of despair sent her to bed where she tossed and turned until her alarm sounded at six. She lay there for a while, one thought chasing another's tail in a foolish game without a winner, before she groaned in frustration and pushed back the duvet. A cool shower refreshed her, but when she looked in the mirror, she saw it hadn't done much for her face. Worse than yesterday, dark circles under her eyes stood out in stark relief against the unusual pallor of her skin. She thought of the series of meetings she had lined up and groaned. It was important to look her best even if she didn't feel it. The careful use of a concealer and heavier make-up made her look a little better – although perhaps a little clownish. She blotted her lipstick and smoothed the make-up along her jawline, took a final look and gave a wry smile. It would have to do.

The day was a nightmare. She struggled with decisions that normally came as second nature to her; the meetings all took longer than expected, and she had a vague idea that she didn't look or sound as confident as she should have done. There were pages and pages of reports to work through, a job she normally enjoyed as she searched for any anomalies but that day she found she needed to read the same paragraph several times before it made sense. The constant need to check her emails didn't help. Despite the notification that came up on the side of her computer screen, every twenty minutes she'd go into the email page on her phone and refresh the screen, just in case. But apart from the usual business emails, there was nothing out of the ordinary.

Nobody was contacting her on her business email address not her personal one. It crossed her mind that she could change it. Belinda, their IT specialist would be able to assign her a new one immediately. But she'd want to know why and any answer Melanie gave, made-up or true, would give rise to the kind of questions she didn't want to answer. She could, of course, remove emails from her phone and wait until she came into work to read them, but she guessed it wouldn't make her life any easier, imagining something was often worse than the reality. Except this reality was bad enough.

With a sigh of frustration, she tried to focus on the reports, scribbling down key points, becoming absorbed in what she was reading despite her worries so that when her phone rang twenty minutes later, it startled her. The junior partners shared an administrative assistant, Rona, an efficient if humourless woman who was skilled at fielding and dealing with calls. If she was putting one through it had to be something work-related, nothing to make her nervous.

Lifting the receiver, she held it to her ear, and said a hesitant, 'Hello?'

'It's Mr Randall for you.'

'Randall?' The name rang a bell but the sound was faint.

'Harry Randall... Fanton's chief accountant.'

She heard the surprise in Rona's voice, the slight note of criticism that Melanie hadn't known the name of someone who would be a major player in the merger negotiations. It was justified censure; every name should be on the tip of her tongue. They normally would be.

The conversation with the accountant was brief and to the point. She hung up, dropped her head into her cupped hands and gave in to a wave of tearfulness before straightening, dabbing her eyes carefully with a tissue and getting on with reading the endless reports. But before she did so, she checked her emails again.

By the next day, she needed to get all the reports read. Everything else was in hand and there was nothing in her diary to distract her; a couple of minor things that needed doing could be done by the two junior associates who were working with her. She quickly emailed both and gave them a rundown of what was required, then sat back, manicured nails tapping on the desk.

An idea had been simmering in the back of her head, it took form and solidified. She could work under pressure; she was used to that, but what she couldn't do was work with this axe hanging over her head waiting to drop and decapitate her at any moment. Overdramatic, maybe, but it was exactly how she felt. She needed to get rid of it and there seemed to be only one way to do that.

Someone knew about her. About Anne Edwards.

She had to go back to where it had started.

Go back to Wethersham and face her past.

6

Melanie had only one day to make her plan work. Before she left the office, she sent an email to Richard Masters telling him that everything was organised and she was going to work from home the next day so she could give her full concentration to reading the various reports. It was acceptable practice; she'd done it as a senior associate but she felt bad that she was lying to him. He'd never know but it didn't make the lie sit any easier.

Of course, she could have told him that she intended to read them on the train. But he'd have asked where she was going, then he'd have asked why. Why would anyone choose to go to the Yorkshire town of Wethersham in February? If he had ever been there, he'd wonder why anyone would want to go there at all. She certainly didn't. Since she and her mother had left, she'd never gone back and when people asked where she was from, she said Shoreham-by-Sea, the West Sussex town they'd fled to almost twenty-five years before.

It had been her mother's decision to leave. She was a small nervous woman, widowed in her early thirties and left with a young daughter for whom she'd never developed any maternal feelings. Following what she referred to ever after as Melanie's disgusting behaviour, she'd been unable to face the neighbours or handle the snide remarks, sideways looks and outright venom from the people in the town. She'd never really forgiven Melanie for the disgrace and embarrassment, nor had she ever settled into the much smaller house they'd been forced to buy in Shoreham. Worse, she'd never let her daughter forget the sacrifices she'd had to make.

But Melanie wasn't going to let anything mess up her promotion. And if going back to that God-forsaken place got her the answers she needed, well then, back she'd go. It might be a complete waste of time but she had to do something, today's gruelling day told her that. This was only the start of the merger process; it was going to get a lot more complicated and difficult once the actual negotiations started and she needed to be able to focus.

Having missed lunch, she was starving by the time she reached home but also too exhausted to think about cooking. She dropped her bag in the hallway and headed out again to the Indian restaurant a few minutes' walk away to pick up a takeaway and a short while later was sitting in her kitchen with aromatic food on a plate in front of her. She'd only eaten a few mouthfuls when she heard the ping from the hallway. It was like a magic spell, she instantly froze with the fork laden with fried rice halfway to her mouth. Then she was released, the fork falling from her fingers, rice tumbling to speckle her navy blouse with spots of grease as it fell. She pushed the plate away. Would *nobody* have answered the question or would this be a new comment to torture her?

She picked up her bag, took out the phone and put it down on the table, sitting to stare at it with worried eyes. Her throat was dry, reaching for her water glass she took a mouthful, swallowing with a loud gulp. The glass rattled on the table as she placed it carefully to one side and reached for the phone with both hands, inhaling noisily as she turned it on and pressed the email icon.

The email didn't say, as she'd almost hoped, *time to pay me a squillion pounds.* Hadn't she known in her heart that it wasn't going to be that simple? It did, however, answer her question. In capitals. Like a scream. *YOU KNOW WHAT FOR ANNE EDWARDS.* The anger in the words was palpable. It made her shiver but at least now she knew exactly what this person wanted.

Revenge. They wanted revenge for what had happened in Wethersham.

It wasn't what she'd wanted to hear but at least they had replied so she chanced another email, another question. There didn't seem to be much point in asking who it was, they were hardly going to tell her, instead, keeping it short she tapped out, *Why now?* Without any real expectation that they'd answer she sat with her eyes glued to the phone for several minutes before dropping it on the table. It wasn't until she'd scraped the food into a bin and put the plate in the dishwasher that she heard the ping. Spinning around, eyes wide, she looked at it. This time there was no hesitation, she switched it on and went to email.

Her eyes widened further when she saw the reply. *Why not.* Not in capitals this time, no, this was a quiet, cruel answer. There had been no reason to reply. Psychological torture. They thought she'd be frightened, that she'd be falling to pieces. They were right about the first, she was damned if they were going to be right about the second.

The answer had to lie in Wethersham.

7

Melanie made the 6am train from King's Cross by seconds, dashing along the platform and climbing in the first open door. The seat she'd booked was the other end of the train, forcing her to struggle through all the carriages, her briefcase bumping her thigh as she negotiated the passageways. Finally, she reached her pre-booked seat only to find someone ensconced in it, a man in such a deep sleep it took strenuous effort to wake him. He wasn't pleased, grunting, groaning and attempting to turn away from her to snuggle back into *her* seat.

'Excuse me,' she said, using her knuckles to push his shoulder harder this time. She could have sat in one of the other empty seats but they were all sporting reserved tickets so somebody could get on at the next station and ask her to move. She didn't want to be disturbed; this might be her only opportunity to get those reports read. 'This is my seat,' she said, when the man reluctantly opened his eyes. She waved her ticket inches from his nose.

Seeing she wasn't going to give up, he huffed and puffed as he shuffled to his feet, giving her filthy looks from under shaggy eyebrows and mumbling imprecations under his breath. He was still muttering, and she would have sworn she'd heard the word *bitch*, when he sat in a seat a few rows further down the carriage. Ignoring him, she settled down, took out her laptop and started to read the reports. It was easier to concentrate on them, not only because she was away from the distractions of the office but because the alternative was to think of Wethersham and the woman she hoped to meet there. Her old friend, Cherry Dunsdale.

Melanie had promised to keep in contact when they'd moved and she had planned to. But as soon as she'd crossed the county line from Yorkshire, as soon as she got away from the condemning eyes and hateful remarks, she'd tried to put Wethersham and all that had happened there behind her. And that included Cherry. She hadn't forgotten her though, and thanks to social media, Melanie knew she still lived in the town. There had, of course, been no need for *her* to move away because despite some rumours about her involvement in what had happened, Cherry had never really been implicated. *Her* name hadn't appeared in the local paper. Accusing, condemning fingers hadn't pointed in *her* direction nor had vicious tongues lashed out at her. Melanie could have told them that the idea had been Cherry's, but young as she was she knew a pathetic *it was her idea* wouldn't have helped her cause. Anyway, it might have been her friend's idea, but Melanie had been the one who'd made it work so beautifully, so damn destructively. Even now, it still made her cringe to think of what she had done.

She'd seen Cherry's Facebook page years before and had been tempted to send a friend request, stopping herself at the last moment. The past, she'd thought at the time, was better left where it was. Unfortunately, now it was leeching into her present and poisoning it. She needed to speak to her to see if she could throw any light on who was responsible.

A little over two hours later, the train reached its destination.

York. Melanie grabbed her bag, shoved her laptop inside and edged her way to the door behind a line of travellers. On the platform she looked around with a puzzled frown feeling strangely disorientated. This was the nearest station to Wethersham, she'd been here many times, but either the years had interfered with her memories or it had changed considerably. It was bigger, grander than she remembered; she'd no recollection of the many shops on the concourse or of it ever being this busy.

Outside, there was a queue for the taxi. She stood in line, glad of a day that was cold but dry and bright. She'd worn a warm jacket and comfortable walking shoes, ready for whatever her hometown wanted to throw at her. She wasn't fifteen anymore; she might be nervous, even scared, but maturity had its advantages. Over the years, she'd learned how to slip on a professional façade, a carefully neutral expression that hid the emotions that rolled and surged behind. It would get her through what lay ahead.

It was only fourteen miles from York to Wethersham but roadworks on the way made it a longer journey and it was forty minutes before the taxi dropped her outside the community college where Cherry taught English and French. Or, at least she had. Melanie wasn't sure how up to date the information she'd read online was. She'd soon find out, but first she had to deal with the sting of old memories as they came flooding back.

The grim, red-bricked building hadn't changed since she'd been a pupil there. Some effort had been made to prettify the entrance; neat, clipped box balls sat in tall pots on either side of the double doors but it was the only bit of greenery around. In her day there had been trees, hedges and flower beds. All had been sacrificed to provide extra parking. The playing fields weren't visible from the front of the long two-storey building and the overall impression was of a bleak institution but she remembered being happy there... until she wasn't.

Feeling suddenly nervous, she turned from the entrance and walked toward a service station she could see a few hundred yards down the road. They were sure to have coffee. She'd buy a cup and gather her thoughts.

The station was busy. In the way of a lot of small towns, it served not only as a petrol station but also as a mini supermarket. She bought a takeaway coffee and stood outside drinking it, her eyes searching for something familiar in a street she would have walked down so many times. But her memories of Wethersham were only ones of pain, nothing else had survived. Finally, when she could delay no longer, when she had to move on and do what she'd come here to do, she dropped her empty cup into the rubbish bin and headed back to the school.

This time, she didn't hesitate, she grasped the long metal handle of the front door and pushed. It had never been locked in her day and, despite changing times, it wasn't now, the door moving easily under her hand. She stepped inside, unable to stop a gasp of disbelief as the time warp made her head spin. Nothing here had changed. The large, high-ceilinged entrance hall, with the reception office to one side, was still covered in the same green-and-cream tiles. Black-framed pictures of graduating classes and former teachers still hung in long rows from the picture rails. She didn't examine them too closely; she didn't want to see a photo of her classmates, or that they hadn't put one up because of her. Or maybe there'd be one with her face photoshopped out. The thought made her shiver.

'Can I help you?'

Dragging herself back to the present, she turned to see a middle-aged woman in a heavy tweed skirt and polo-neck jumper standing in the doorway of the office looking at her suspiciously.

Tucking a strand of hair behind her ear, Melanie gave a suddenly anxious laugh. 'Hi, sorry, I was admiring the photographs.' It was such a patent lie that she wasn't surprised when the woman's eyebrows rose in mistrust. 'Actually,' Melanie hurried to explain, 'I was wondering if it would be possible to see Cherry Dunsdale?'

The change in the woman's expression was shocking, disbelief morphing instantly to deep sadness. Only one thing could cause such an expression of sorrow. Melanie's hand rose automatically to her mouth and she held it there, reading the truth in the woman's eyes. The question was almost redundant but Melanie asked it anyway. 'She's dead?'

Rather than answering, the woman waved her into the small office behind. 'Please, come in, sit down. This is obviously a shock.'

Doing as she was bid, feeling too numb to do anything else, Melanie followed her and sat onto the chair indicated, dropping her bag at her feet and folding her arms across her body. Cherry was dead. Regret flooded her, bringing tears to her eyes, a lump to her throat.

'My name is Imelda Lee,' the woman said, taking her seat behind the desk. 'I'm the school administrator. I knew Cherry for a long time, her death was quite a shock.' She struggled to smile. 'It still is, if I'm honest.'

Melanie was used to thinking on her feet, to being faced with seemingly insurmountable problems and she was rarely fazed by anything that was thrown at her, but this had her searching for words in a brain that seemed to have stalled.

It must have been obvious, Imelda stood and moved to where a small kettle sat on top of a metal filing cabinet. With a quick shake to check there was water in it, she switched it on. 'Tea always seems to be a good idea at times like this,' she said gently and said no more until the tea was made. 'Milk and sugar?'

Melanie had been lost in regrets, remembering the pale-faced auburn-haired friend of her youth, wondering if they would have remained friends had things been different. She looked up with a blink when the question was repeated. 'Sorry, milk please.'

'It's UHT, I'm afraid,' Imelda said, putting a mug of tea in front of her and two sachets of milk beside it.

Melanie hated the stuff, would have preferred black coffee but it was too late... it was all too late. She tore the top off one sachet and poured it in. It barely coloured the tea so she added the second. Maybe she should have asked for sugar. Isn't that what they recommended for shock or was that an old wives' tale?

'Are you all right?'

Was she? She wasn't sure, her head was spinning. She'd come seeking answers, hoping that Cherry would be able to help. Sadly, she wasn't sure if the sorrow she felt was for her old friend or for herself. 'It's a shock. What happened to her?' She saw Imelda's hesitation and added, 'We were friends, a long time ago. We'd lost touch but I was coming to surprise her.' It was almost the truth. Twenty-five years since she'd last seen her. She guessed Cherry would have been shocked rather than surprised.

'I may as well tell you because you could find out easily enough from others. People,' Imelda sniffed disparagingly, 'are always willing to gossip and to believe the worst, but it wasn't true, none of it.'

Melanie, expecting to hear a story of a long illness bravely fought, a sudden diagnosis and quick death or a tragic accident, was taken aback. 'I don't understand.'

A deep breath, then on an exhale, three shocking words. 'She committed suicide.' The words fell into the room and floated in the silence before fading. Imelda brushed away the tear that ran down her cheek and sniffed. 'It was a terrible time. She'd worked here as a teacher for over ten years before being promoted to head of department, then before Christmas the school principal retired and she was offered the post.' Imelda lifted her mug and drank deeply before continuing. 'She was so excited, you know, it was her opportunity to make the changes she'd wanted to for years, to build the school up. Ofsted rates us as *good*.' She smiled sadly. 'Cherry's aim was to bring us up to *outstanding*.'

The sadness of loss swept over Melanie. She'd known Cherry the child, she'd never known the woman. She sounded like the kind of person she'd want for a friend, what a shame she'd waited too long. 'What happened?' she asked when the silence stretched uncomfortably long.

Imelda's eyes glistened. 'She was only in the role a few days when it started.' She sighed and cleared her throat noisily. 'Someone posted on Twitter that she'd been seen kissing one of the students. One of the female students,' she added as if that made it, somehow, so much worse. 'Within a few days, graffiti appeared in the students' toilets alleging...' Imelda gulped. '...all kinds of disgusting sexual acts. The maintenance department couldn't keep up with removing them. Cherry laughed it off at first but then the graffiti started appearing around town, on the side of buildings, on the bus shelters. When emails were sent to the board of governors alleging a cover-up, all hell broke loose and she was suspended.'

Tentacles of horror circled Melanie and tightened as she listened. 'A whispering campaign,' she said quietly.

Imelda gave a brief smile. 'Prior to social media that's exactly what it would have been called. The odd whisper here and there gathering momentum, spreading like a nasty fungus. But now, between Twitter and Facebook trolls it is so much more vicious.'

'But there was no truth in any of the allegations?'

Imelda shook her head angrily. 'Of course there wasn't, and when an attempt was made to discover who this girl was that she'd supposedly kissed, well, you won't be surprised to hear that nobody knew, it was all smoke and mirrors. We were able to identify some of the people who tweeted but when questioned, they said they were simply retweeting stuff they'd seen.' Imelda's voice wobbled as she finished, her chin sinking into her polo neck.

'She was fired?'

'Yes. The board of governors said they'd lost confidence in her. They told her that even if the allegations were disproved, people would always wonder, and there would be those who would maintain that there was no smoke without fire. I think,' Imelda said, her voice thick with tears, 'that it was the *even if* that finished her. She told me later that her heart had ripped in two when she heard the doubt in their voices.'

Melanie stared at Imelda without blinking. 'So, she killed herself.'

'Sleeping tablets. She had a problem with occasional periods of insomnia and had been taking them on and off for years. It seems she'd built up quite a collection; when they found her there were several empty packets beside her.' Imelda didn't brush away the tears this time, they ran down her cheeks and dropped to her jumper. 'Cherry was a dedicated teacher who really cared about the pupils. It was a shocking, tragic waste and I hope whoever started those rumours rots in hell.'

Melanie wanted to leave, wanted to run from the school and from Wethersham, much as she had done all those years before, but she wasn't sure her legs would support her. Luckily, Imelda seemed to understand. 'You've had a bad shock.'

A worse shock than she realised. Melanie kept her eyes fixed on the floor in front of her, afraid to look up in case Imelda saw the terror in them. Because, of course, she knew who'd started the rumours about Cherry, the same person who was sending her the emails. She'd been right, somebody wanted to exact revenge for what happened twenty-five years earlier.

'Are you feeling okay, you've gone terribly pale.' The words broke into her thoughts.

Melanie looked up. She guessed what she was feeling showed on her face because Imelda suddenly looked worried, her eyelids fluttering nervously as she looked at her, then down at papers on the desk. 'I really need to get back to work,' she said, picking up a letter.

'Yes, of course, thank you for your time.' Melanie stood and gave a shaky smile before turning and walking from the office.

Outside, the day had turned grey and chilly, dark clouds low in the sky hinting at heavy rain to come. It matched a mood that had swung from horrified to angry determination.

Whoever was doing this, whoever had broken Cherry, Melanie was damned if that person was going to break her.

8

Melanie wasn't tempted to visit any of her old haunts. There was nothing in Wethersham she wanted to see, the good times of her early youth had been devoured by those last agonising months of pointing fingers and hostility. And yet, as she trudged the twenty-minute walk to the town centre, she imagined she heard innocent and hopeful childish voices floating on the breeze, hers and Cherry's, echoes of those early times she'd forgotten. A heavy weight of regret weighed her down; not only for what she'd done but for what she hadn't, for the friendship she'd let go too easily. Now it was too late.

She half expected the town centre, like the train station, to have changed, but it looked exactly the same, if maybe a little smaller, a tad shabbier. The town hall too, looked less imposing than she remembered but she was pleased to see the taxi rank was still outside, and more than relieved to see a taxi waiting.

'York train station,' she said to the driver and slid into the back seat. She shut her eyes as it pulled away, relieved to be leaving Wethersham and making a silent promise never to return.

The roadworks seemed to have mysteriously disappeared so

within twenty minutes the taxi was pulling up outside the train station. Melanie checked her phone and was stunned to see it was only eleven forty-five. She'd expected to be in Wethersham for most of the day, maybe having lunch with Cherry, catching up, sorting out her dilemma. Now, Melanie's heart twisting with remorse, she stood outside the station wondering what she was going to do. She'd booked tickets on the five o'clock train home but she had no reason to hang around. Inside, she peered up at the timetable, relieved to see there was one she could catch in an hour.

An hour. She headed back out to the street and looked around. Away from the deadening influence of Wethersham, she was able to concentrate on the chilling thought that someone had deliberately and callously destroyed Cherry. Was that what they were trying to do to her now? Shivering, she pulled the collar of her coat up and shoved her hands into her pockets. It was a bitterly chilly day but she knew it wasn't the weather that was making her cold inside.

A pub sign caught her eye. A drink seemed like a good solution. It would warm her up, take the edge off the tension and might help clear her mind. She waited for a gap in the traffic and dashed across.

Inside the pub it was warm and cosy. There was only one other customer in the far corner with a pint of something dark in his hand, a newspaper spread out over the small table in front of him holding his attention. A lone bartender stood behind the bar, lazily polishing the gleaming surface, a slight smile indicating his mind was elsewhere. He looked up and raised an enquiring eyebrow when she approached.

Melanie frowned and eyed the bottles behind him before deciding to throw herself on his mercy. 'I've had a bit of a shit morning and need something to take the edge off it all,' she said bluntly.

Maybe it wasn't such an unusual request because he stared at her for a moment before turning to scan the row of bottles behind him. He reached for one, took a small glass and poured honey-coloured liquid into it. 'Lagavulin,' he said. 'It's whisky, designed to hit whatever ails you.'

She paid what seemed to be a large amount of money for a short drink and took it to a seat near the open fire. Lifting it to her nose, she sniffed. It smelt of smoke and peat. Tentatively, she sipped, surprised to find it tasted the same. It didn't exactly hit what ailed her, but a few sips took the edge off the despair that was washing over her in waves.

Somebody wanted revenge. Melanie had hoped Cherry would have been able to help her but it seemed she couldn't even help herself. She wondered if along with the tweets and the scurrilous graffiti, Cherry had received emails similar to those she'd had. Her eyes narrowed in thought before she shook her head. No, she didn't think so. Cherry wasn't stupid; if she'd got the emails, she'd have done exactly what Melanie had done, she'd have gone looking for her. Melanie had made herself hard to find, but not impossible.

With the whisky an antidote to the chill inside and the fire warming her fingers and toes, she considered her options. There weren't many. In fact, only one. There was one other person who might be able to help. Not a friend and someone she hadn't seen since she left Wethersham. She hadn't ever wanted to see him again. But she seemed to be out of choices.

Eric Thomas. The mere thought of the name poured icy water on the whisky warmth, quenching it in an instant. She looked at her almost empty glass and was tempted to get another, wondering vaguely if this was how it would end with her, a drinking habit to enable her to cope. Shutting her eyes briefly, she sighed. Eric Thomas. She barely knew him; his family had moved from Leeds to Wethersham only a few months before everything had fallen apart. He'd been a year above her in school, a year at that tender age making a big difference. Taller and broader, she remembered he'd seemed like a man in comparison to the boys in her year.

After she and her mother had fled Wethersham, she'd heard nothing of him or of anyone she'd left behind. Her mother refused to maintain contacts with old friends or neighbours; too embarrassed and ashamed, too mired in bitterness that soured her until the massive heart attack that had taken her suddenly, leaving Melanie, despite everything, bereft.

When she'd found Cherry on Facebook, years before, Melanie had peered at the photographs that were there for all to see. Cherry with friends, in the school, at various functions. Melanie had scanned the other people in the group shots, seeing nobody familiar until she saw Eric in the background of one taken at a sponsored charity run. She'd recognised him straight away, the same neat, rather old-fashioned haircut, the same intense stare as he looked into the camera. Curious, she'd done a few internet searches and discovered he lived in London, in Edgware which wasn't that many miles from where she'd lived at the time. She'd liked to have known more about him but didn't risk doing a friend request. He wouldn't have recognised her name but she'd worked too hard to separate her past from who she had become, she wasn't willing to risk blending the two together again. As a result, she hadn't found any personal details, only that he worked as a car salesman in a local dealership. She'd not bothered to narrow it down to one, she'd no idea then that she'd ever need to know.

But she had to face it; with Cherry dead, he might well be her only hope.

He might also be nobody.

That thought came thundering out of the dark and jolted her. Strangely, stupidly perhaps, she'd not considered it, but of course it was true. Eric, after all, had every reason to hate her and plenty of reason to want revenge. But why would he wait until now? She threw back the last of the whisky. It was something she could ask him when she found him, because she was damned if she was going to sit around and wait to see what he was going to do. She'd find him and confront him.

Tapping the side of the empty glass with a fingernail, she cursed herself for not having found out exactly where he worked. Edgware was a big place, there were likely to be several car dealerships and she didn't have the luxury of time to enable her to trawl through them all. With one final tap on the glass, a thought came to her. She knew who she could ask for help. Masters used a small private investigation service to help with the more difficult traces and to investigate the dodgier of their clients with discretion. They could do, in a short while, what might very well take her hours, time she wouldn't have to spare over the next couple of days.

Thinking of work, a twinge of guilt hit her. She hadn't checked her emails all morning and she wouldn't have heard its alerts with all the surrounding noise. There might very well be some waiting for her attention. With a reluctant sigh, she fished in her bag for her phone and put it on the ring-marked table beside her empty glass. Another whisky would make looking at it a little easier. She shook her head at the thought and picked up her phone to check.

There were three emails from the associates who were working with her on the merger. Simple questions that nevertheless required an answer. It didn't take long, a simple, *yes, please,* a *no, that's fine, don't worry about it* and *no, leave it and I'll sort it when I get back*. With work, for the moment, sorted, she scrolled through her list of contacts to find the private investigator's number. This was the best course of action, wasn't it? Gritting her teeth, she pressed ring. It was her *only* course of action.

'Rabbie and Henderson.'

No mention of what they did, such was their level of discretion. 'Hi, it's Melanie Scott from Masters Corporate Law, may I speak with Alistair, please?'

Considering the amount of work they put their way, she wasn't surprised when she was put through immediately. She'd met Alistair once, a short, skinny Scot, who was blunt to the point of rudeness but with an engaging smile that meant people weren't quite sure if their leg weren't being pulled, ever so gently. 'Ms Scott, what can I do for you?'

'I need information about someone,' she said and gave him Eric Thomas's name. 'I know he works for a car dealership in Edgware, I need to know which one.'

'E.R.I.C?' He spelled out the name, his intonation rising in a question mark at the end.

Did it matter? She bit back the words; he was giving the request the same amount of attention he always did; it wasn't his fault she was more personally invested this time. 'That's it,' she said.

'Okay. I'll put Liam on it.'

'Liam?' Another name, another person involved. 'Can't you do it?'

There was an infinitesimal pause before Alistair replied. 'Liam has done quite a bit of work for Masters since he started with us three months ago. He's an ex-copper. Solid and reliable. If you've heard otherwise...?

She hadn't. But Alistair had put her on the back foot while skilfully avoiding her question. 'No. Of course I haven't.'

'Fine,' he said, as if that was that. 'I'll fill him in and he'll get back to you with the information you require as soon as it's available.'

And with that she had to be satisfied. 'Send the invoice to me personally,' she added. She didn't anticipate her request being queried and it wasn't.

'Fine,' Alistair said again, as if this was the norm.

It was as simple as that. She put her phone back into her bag, gave a wave of thanks to the bartender and made her way back to the station with a few minutes to spare before her train was due.

9

Unfortunately, Melanie didn't manage to get a seat with a table on the journey home and had to make do with a flip-down table that was hardly fit for purpose. Propping her laptop up as best as she could, she ploughed through the reports she needed to read for the following day, sighing as she lost focus after a few paragraphs, her thoughts drifting to Cherry and to what had happened.

Something suddenly puzzled her and she sat back and stared out the window. Whoever was responsible had made up a scandal to disgrace Cherry, but they didn't need to make up one to destroy her. It was there, waiting. So why didn't they use it? Or, she frowned, was that the next step? Were they torturing her by dragging out the inevitable disclosure? Maybe she'd arrive at the meeting tomorrow, or the more important one with the two CEOs on Friday and see strained faces and a disgusted, disappointed look in eyes that refused to meet hers. There'd be nudges, whispers, conversations that died when she walked into a room and barely disguised sniggers. Her belly knotted at the thought of going through it all again. Last time, she'd been a child, she didn't think being an adult would make it any easier.

She pulled out her mobile and checked her emails again. Nothing.

With a gulp and a frustrated shake of her head, she tried once again to concentrate on the reports and managed to get through most of them before the train pulled into King's Cross.

She'd have liked the comfort of a taxi to take her home but she settled for the speed and efficiency of the tube. It was a mere ten minutes' walk from the nearest station to her apartment, a short walk on a dry day, a long, long way when the rain was coming down in a deluge that darkened the day, blurred the edges of the city she knew and soaked through her coat within seconds. By the time her damp fingers fumbled with the key to her front door she was wet, weary and more than a little anxious.

In the hallway, she kicked off her shoes and padded into the kitchen, leaving curiously-shaped patches behind her on the pale wooden floor. Her coat was wet through, she peeled it off and threw it over the back of a chair before eyeing the dark patches on her shirt in disgust. Her showerproof coat was most definitely not British rainproof. She took a step towards the doorway, stopping to turn and slip her laptop from her briefcase, setting it up on the kitchen table and plugging it in to charge. It would be ready to go whenever she got back to it. Unable to resist, she checked her phone again. One email from one of the associates, acknowledging her earlier email. Nothing else.

She'd half-expected one from Hugo. Friday. It was only two days away, wasn't he going to contact her to... how had he put it... *firm up arrangements*. His last email had given her so much hope, had she been fooling herself? She gave a dismissive shrug that developed too quickly into a defeated slump as that thought took hold. It would crush her if she let it.

Deciding that being cold and hungry didn't help her mood,

she rang her local Italian restaurant and ordered a takeaway. She hung up on the promise it would arrive within fifteen minutes and headed into her bedroom to change into a brushed jersey sweatshirt and leggings. Comfortable but still feeling miserable, she found it impossible to resist the temptation to check again for emails. This time, to her surprise, there was one from Hugo. The earlier defeatist thought was still ringing in her ears and she hesitated. Was he emailing to cancel? Only one way to find out. She tapped the email icon and watched as the words appeared, blinking in pleasure when she read, *Looking forward to Friday. I can pick you up, if you like.*

She read it twice, her mood instantly lifting. And then more doubt piled in. If he picked her up wouldn't it follow that he'd take her home? So, did the offer come with an expectation? She hadn't wanted to play games but it seemed like she'd been co-opted into this *will he/won't he, should she/shouldn't she* tango.

It wasn't a good time to waste energy playing mating games. On Friday, she had the meeting with the CEOs of the two financial institutions involved in this merger. It was a key meeting; and likely to be a stressful day. Maybe it wasn't a good idea to meet Hugo that day, she would cancel.

She tapped out a short message. *Unfortunately, I'm very busy, maybe we could make it another night?* and pressed send before she could change her mind.

The phone clasped in her hand, she waited for him to reply. She was caught between conflicting desires, one that he would accept it as a brush-off and leave her alone and one that wanted him to insist, to say how much he'd been looking forward to it, to ask, *What about Saturday or Sunday or any day, he had to see her.* She was giggling at her childish ridiculousness when the phone pinged, dragging her eyes to the screen.

You still need to eat, and we could be home early if you want.

It wasn't even close to what she'd hoped to read, and the *we could be home early* almost made her groan as she wondered exactly what he meant by it. Okay, bottom line, did she want to see him or not? She shook her head, it was a silly question, of course she did, even an email from him had sent her heart racing. Doing a quick internet search on her laptop, she tapped out an answer. *True, I do need to eat. It's easier if I meet you. At the Spanish restaurant, at eight.* She added the postcode and sent the email with a faint smile.

Standing waiting for his reply, her attention fixed on the phone, the sound of the doorbell startled her and she spun around, eyes wide, heart beating, fear a painful lump in her throat. Only when it rang a second time did she remember the takeaway she'd ordered. 'Idiot,' she said, picking up her purse and heading to answer the door.

Returning with the bag, she put it on the countertop before checking her phone, smiling in satisfaction as she read his reply. *Fine, see you then.* It was, she knew, stupid to be so elated by his emails and she was annoyed with herself at his ability to affect her mood. It would have been better to have stood her ground and cancelled dinner, but as she ate the food she'd ordered, her mind was on what to wear for their second date.

After dinner, she settled down to finish reading the reports, but found herself distracted by thoughts of Hugo and Friday night. He wasn't picking her up, but might he want to drop her home? Was she reading too much into the *we could be home early*? With her mind constantly wandering, it was nearly midnight by the time she was done with the reports. Then, exhausted, she climbed into bed and fell instantly into a heavy sleep, not waking until her alarm went off the next morning.

To her intense satisfaction, her hard work paid off and the meetings arranged for the day went as she'd planned. There was no question she was unable to answer; no issue arose that she couldn't discuss. By the end of the day, she was exhausted but completely satisfied with how everything had gone. 'Well done,' she said to the associates who'd been so diligent. 'We make a good team.'

But it had been a long day. It was nearly seven before she was ready to leave and she still had to read some reports that had been sent to her during the day. Her eyes were gritty, she didn't fancy another few hours staring at the computer screen so she printed them out, sighing when she lifted the sheaf of papers. More than she'd expected, it would be another late night.

She stopped at a deli on the way home to get something to eat, then settled herself at the kitchen table with the reports in front of her, a sandwich on one side and a mug of tea on the other. An hour later, she rubbed her eyes wearily and stood to get a drink of water. She had turned on the tap and was holding the glass underneath when her phone pinged to tell her she'd another email. She stood staring at it, water spilling over the rim of the glass and running down her arm to wet the sleeve of her shirt.

A slight flicker of optimism – maybe it was Hugo – was quickly brushed aside. She knew who it was. She picked up a towel and dried her hand, dabbing the wet sleeve, her eyes fixed on the phone. Finally, she picked it up.

If there'd been a shadow of a doubt in her mind that Cherry's death was part of someone's idea of revenge, it disappeared when she read the short email. *Your friend died too quickly.*

'Bastard!' she cried, dropping the phone on the table, and turning away from it to pace the room. It was one thing, to suspect that someone had deliberately driven Cherry to her death, another entirely to be faced with the truth. *Too quickly*. Was that the reason for this campaign of torture? Terror dug its sharp claws into her head. She stumbled to the chair, rested her elbows on the table and dropped her face into her hands.

It was a few minutes before she moved, and only then because she remembered a gift she'd been given a few years before. She went into the living room and rummaged in the cupboard until she found it – a bottle of whisky she'd never opened. She splashed some into a glass and sank onto a chair. It wasn't as smoky or smooth as the whisky she'd had in York and she coughed as it hit the back of her throat. But when the glass was empty, she felt calmer. There was no need to stop at one, she wasn't going anywhere. After the third, she stopped counting, the fear and gut-spasming terror fading with every sip.

When she woke in the morning, it was to a mind-blowing headache that made her groan before opening her eyes to see a stretch of cream carpet in front of her. She blinked, disorientated as she struggled to sit. The chair she'd been sitting on was on its side, the half-empty whisky bottle still upright beside it. Whimpering, she straightened the chair and used it to get to her feet, immediately dropping onto it and shutting her eyes as the room spun. She allowed a few minutes' wallow in self-pity before struggling to her feet again and heading to the kitchen. There was nothing in her limited supply of medication to effect a quick remedy for a hangover so she settled for a couple of painkillers, hoping to take the edge off the pounding headache. She swallowed them down with a glass of water and forced herself to drink another.

It was only seven. She had time to effect a transformation from a miserable wreck into something closer to a corporate lawyer in the middle of sensitive negotiations. She didn't look at the email again. It wasn't necessary. *Your friend died too quickly*. The words were seared into her soul.

She peeled off her clothes and stepped into the shower, running it cool in the hope it would clear her head. It was a slim hope that didn't pay out. She stepped out and wrapped a towel around herself, avoiding the bathroom mirror as she did so. She didn't want to see the fear that might twist her expression.

By the time she was dressed, the painkillers were beginning to dull the throb in her head. She applied her makeup, acknowledging the troubled look in her eyes as she did so. It would, she hoped, pass as understandable concern for the meetings that day but she needed to put the email out of her head until she'd heard from Rabbie and Henderson. She was pinning her hopes on Eric Thomas being the key. Either he was responsible or he'd know who was. When she got the information she needed, she'd plan her next step. Until then, she needed to focus on the job. She *would* focus on her job. She wasn't going to let the crippling fear destroy her or ruin all she'd worked so hard for.

Whoever was doing this, they were going to learn she was made of tougher stuff than Cherry.

10

Had Melanie been a regular heavy drinker she'd have taken extra precautions. She'd have sucked mints on the way to work and would certainly have avoided meeting anyone important for the first hour or two. But she wasn't, and when she saw Richard Masters outside their office building, she waved a greeting and fell into step beside him. Outside in the cool, rather breezy morning it was fine but in the close confines of the lift she quickly became aware of something she should have known – her breath still stank of alcohol. She stopped talking, kept her mouth shut and breathed in and out through her nose.

When the lift opened at her floor, she stepped out before turning. 'Have a good day,' she said, her heart plummeting when she saw him regarding her with narrowed eyes and a pinched mouth that said clearly he was disappointed in her.

In her office she shut the door and searched in the top drawer of her desk for the toothpaste she kept there. Squirting an inch of it onto her finger, she rubbed it around her teeth, licked it off, squished it around her mouth and swallowed. Afraid that her office would smell of stale alcohol, she pushed the window up the two inches security precautions allowed and wedged the door open to create a draught. Her first meeting, a simple catch-up with the two junior associates, wasn't until eleven. It would be fine by then.

There was a chilled water dispenser in the staffroom. She filled a paper cup and drank it down in frantic gulps, sipped a second more slowly and took two back with her to drink while she worked.

Fear was never far from the surface and a notification that she had a new email made it spike and send her heart pounding. Her fingers froze on the keyboard and she stared at it unblinking for several seconds. Then with a dart of bravado she clicked on the email icon.

It was from Hugo. Her shoulders slumped with relief as she read the brief message. *Looking forward to seeing you again tonight.* The self-doubt that always haunted her faded, and a tingle of pleasure shot through her as she thought of the evening ahead. She was so glad she hadn't cancelled. After a stressful night and the meetings planned for that day, dinner with a handsome, charming man was exactly what she needed. It was what she deserved. She hesitated over her reply, searching for the right words. With a sigh she settled for the simple, *Me too, see you at eight.*

She switched off notifications on her computer. If another email came, she didn't want to know.

The afternoon meeting with the CEOs of Fanton's and CityEast, John Backhoe and Deanne Sandler, was held in the conference room and went as Melanie had anticipated. It was a preliminary meeting, there were no surprises and no questions she couldn't answer. In the end, she was satisfied with how things were going forward. Exhausted from the effort of concentrating, she hid her relief when each of the CEOs cited pressures of work for declining her offer of lunch.

'Another time, perhaps,' Melanie said, picking up the reports she'd been discussing with them and returning them to the file.

'Perhaps we could celebrate when it's all done,' Deanne said, picking up her briefcase. 'It all seems to be going very smoothly.'

Melanie made polite chit-chat as she walked with them to reception and waited until they'd left before returning to her office. She dropped the file on her desk before flopping onto her chair. It would have been nice to have put her head down and sleep... just for ten minutes... instead, she pulled her laptop towards her and concentrated on getting the details of the meeting on record. Her fingers were flying across the keyboard when her phone rang. One hand snaked out to pick it up without taking her eyes from the computer screen. 'Melanie Scott.'

It was Rona. 'There's a Liam Quinn here to see you.' Her voice was laced with curiosity. 'He doesn't have an appointment but he insists on speaking with you.'

Liam Quinn? *Liam?* 'Ah yes,' Melanie said quickly. 'Yes, that's fine, send him in.' With a final glance at the screen, she exited and switched the computer off. It was almost five, she was exhausted. She'd see what this Liam had to say and head home. After all, she had a date.

'Come in,' she called when a knock signalled the private investigator's arrival, her eyes fixed expectantly on the door as it was pushed open. An ex-policeman, Alistair had said, so the broad, muscular build wasn't surprising. Neither were the sharp, rather cold, grey eyes that swept over her.

Then Quinn smiled and his stern expression instantly softened. 'Hi,' he said, shutting the door behind him.

Melanie stood and held out her hand. It was caught in his warm, surprisingly soft one and shaken once before being dropped. 'Please, have a seat.' She indicated the chair behind him.

He drew it closer to the desk, sat and shoved his hands into the pockets of his jacket, his eyes never leaving her face. A lock of dark, curly hair streaked with grey fell over his forehead. He tossed it back with a jerk of his head. 'You look like you've had a hard day.'

There was no sympathy in his voice, merely an assessment. It wasn't the kind of thing any woman wanted to hear and irritation swept over her. 'It has been a busy day. Now,' she said, crossing her arms, 'I assume you've come with the information I requested.'

'Not big into pleasantries, are we?' He reached into his inside pocket, took out a folded piece of paper and handed it to her.

'Thank you.' Melanie opened the note and stared at the words scrawled across it. *Edgware Motors, Watford Way*. 'This is where Eric Thomas works?'

'For the last six years.'

She folded the piece of paper again, smoothing the edges with her fingers. Eric was her last hope. Facing him after all these years... even the thought of it appalled her. The idea that he might be responsible for the emails horrified her because, if he were, how could she criticise him after what she had done? And yet, wouldn't it be easier if it were him? It would be logical, understandable even. If it weren't, it meant someone she didn't know hated her and that unknown was even more terrifying.

Something of her dilemma must have been obvious because Quinn leaned forward, his grey eyes boring into her. 'Are you all right?'

She managed a shaky smile. 'Yes, sorry, it has been an unusually tough day.' He said nothing and she felt herself relax.

In a world that had seemed a little shaky recently, there was something solid and reassuring about his presence and she felt a lessening of the bands of tension that had been wrapped around her all day. This was what she needed, someone else's strength for a while, a brace for her backbone until it mended.

No, she quickly corrected herself and lifted her chin. Her backbone wasn't broken, just a little worn. She wasn't a helpless female, dependant on a man to get her through the bad times, she never had been and she wasn't going to start now. This madness would get sorted and everything would be all right. She stood and held out her hand. 'Thank you again, Mr Quinn.'

His warm hand enveloped hers. He held it for longer than was customary as his eyes, harder now, seemed to search hers. She was about to object when he let her go and reached into his jacket pocket. 'In case you need to contact me directly,' he said, handing her a business card. 'You can get me on that number, at any time.'

When he'd gone, she put the card into her purse, opened the piece of paper he'd given her again and used her phone to do an internet search for Edgware Motors. It was open the following morning. There was no point in putting it off. She was convinced that Eric Thomas was either responsible for the emails or would know who was. The *why after all these years* was something else. There was no point in trying to second-guess the unguessable.

At home, she dropped her briefcase on the floor in the lounge and sank onto the sofa. Despite his earlier email, she was so tired that if Hugo weren't as close to perfect as she'd met in a while, she'd have considered putting him off until another night. But she didn't want to mess this up. *As she always did*. Batting her mother's voice away, Melanie headed to her bedroom. Tonight, there was no desire to wear fancy underwear or a slinky, tight-fitting dress. She didn't even bother to unpin her hair before having a shower. Hugo could drop her home but if he had any hope of more it was doomed to failure, she was way too tired. With the idea that he might get the message, she dressed for comfort and convenience, pulling on a pair of stretch jeans and a pale-blue cashmere jumper and leaving her hair as it was. She remembered Quinn's comment from earlier and wondered if Hugo too would comment that it looked as if she'd had a hard day.

The taxi she'd ordered arrived on time and she reached the restaurant at ten to eight. Pleased she'd arrived first, she was shown to a table towards the back of the busy restaurant and took a seat facing the door to watch for Hugo's arrival. Nervous anticipation fizzled through her. She looked down at her jumper, sorry she hadn't worn something else or at least added some jewellery. Why hadn't she made more of an effort? The only thing she could think to do was to pull strands of hair down from her tight chignon and curl them around her fingers before releasing. She debated going to the ladies to check it looked okay, deciding against because, after all, what could she do if it weren't? Reminding herself that at her age she should have more sense, she ordered a bottle of sparkling water and sipped a glass as she waited, her eyes glued to the door for the first sight of Hugo.

He arrived at a minute to eight, striding through the door, exuding confidence. She had a few seconds to observe him, surprised that his features looked harder than she remembered, his eyes colder, with none of the warmth that had so appealed to her. But when he saw her, his face lit up and he hurried over to bend and kiss her cheek. 'You were early!'

'Traffic was light,' she said, smiling at him. In the stress of the week she'd had, she'd forgotten how gorgeous he was.

He shook his head as he took the seat opposite. 'I would have picked you up, you know.'

'Yes, thank you, but a taxi was okay.'

If he understood exactly why she'd been reticent about his picking her up, he made no comment. Instead, he tilted his head and looked at her with a concerned narrowing of his brown eyes. 'If you don't mind me saying so, you look as though you've had a tough week.'

She laughed. 'You're not the first person to have said that today.'

'Tell me,' he said. 'It's good to talk, you know.'

The truth wasn't an option so Melanie gave an explanation he could understand. 'I had a tough meeting. It went very well but as a result I have a lot of information buzzing around my head.' Then, because part of her brain was still in work mode, she added, 'At least I'll have the weekend to go through all the reports.'

'You're going to be staring at a computer screen all weekend?' Hugo looked horrified at the thought. 'That doesn't sound like fun.'

'Actually, I enjoy what I do, and making sure I have every point clear in my head will make things much easier as the merger progresses.'

'Oh, this is the merger of the two finance institutions you were telling me about last week.' He smiled. 'You see, I was listening! I suppose the details take a long time to work out. It's going to be tiring for you.' He reached a hand across the table and grasped hers.

Melanie felt her colour rise as his thumb gently stroked her skin.

Hugo withdrew his hand as the waiter bustled over to take their order. Since neither had looked at the menu, he went away again and for the next few minutes the conversation was about which dishes to choose. Decisions made, conversation became more general and Melanie felt herself relaxing more as the evening went on. The food was good, the man opposite... well, he was perfect.

'I've had a commission to design a house in Slovakia,' Hugo said, making her heart sink. 'I'll be heading over for an initial consultation on Tuesday, then I'll spend a few weeks drawing up the plans. It's my favourite part of the process.'

'So, you'll be back and forward a few times?'

'That's the way it goes. A couple of days next week, a couple of days when the plans are ready. Once building starts, I'll probably stay for about a week and after that I'll visit as needed, depending on progress or whether there are any unforeseen issues.' Pushing his plate away, he picked up his wine glass. 'Why don't you come with me one of the times? I'll be busy during the day but the evenings will be free. It's very pretty there, you'd like it.'

'I'm sure I would,' Melanie said, pleased, if slightly taken aback by the invitation. 'Unfortunately, I'm going to be tied up with this merger.' She was flattered by the flicker of regret she saw. They'd only known each other a week but she suddenly felt as if they'd known each other forever and her life was filling with possibilities. Slovakia, why not? 'We don't anticipate any problems with the merger. Both companies want it to be expedited and everything is proving straightforward. The negotiations should be complete within another week, two at the outside. Maybe I could go with you then?'

'A couple of weeks?' He smiled and reached for her hand again. 'That would be perfect.'

Feeling more relaxed than she had in a long time, Melanie smiled at him and laughed at his jokes. She might even have fluttered her eyelashes. It all felt so right. 'I must give you my phone number,' she said, opening her bag to take out a business card. She wrote her number clearly across the back of it. 'Now you can text or ring, if you want to.'

'Thank you,' he said, taking the card. He took out his phone and tapped in her number. 'Much more personal than emails.'

'It's a bit quicker,' she said, trying to brush it off, feeling colour flash across her cheeks at the look in his eyes when he looked up from his mobile. Then she heard hers ping.

'Now you have my number too,' Hugo said. He reached across the table to clasp her hand. 'Poor you, you look exhausted. We should go and I'll drive you home, no argument.'

Hugo put his arm around her shoulder, holding her close to him as they walked the short distance to his car. There wasn't much said, the silence deliciously comfortable, the silence of old friends, of lovers. He put her address in his satnav and followed the directions to her apartment. It took a few minutes to find parking, then he turned to her. 'I know you're tired but I don't want the evening to end yet. How about a coffee?' He reached out a finger and trailed it slowly down her cheek. 'Then, if you want me to, I'll leave you to get your beauty sleep.'

If you want me to. She was so tired but, like him, she didn't want the evening to end. 'Coffee would end the evening nicely,' she said, and with his arm around her again, they walked to her apartment. It had been a long time since she'd been out with anyone special. Truth was, in the last couple of years it had been a series of fleeting relationships that had filled a gap and left a hole.

'This is a very nice place you have,' Hugo said as she opened the front door.

It was warm inside, a table lamp casting a soft glow over the hallway. They stood close enough that she could smell his cologne, a rich spicy scent she didn't recognise. Her breath caught as he bent his head and kissed her cheek, his lips moving down to the hollow of her neck. 'You're so beautiful,' he said, leaning back to look at her.

Melanie's tiredness washed away on a wave of desire. 'And you are incredibly handsome,' she whispered, reaching a hand up to lay it against his cheek.

There was no more talk of coffee.

11

Melanie felt warm breath on her cheeks and the touch of his lips. 'I have to go,' Hugo said. 'It's early, don't stir, I'll ring you later.'

Through half-opened eyes she could see the room was in darkness, no light creeping around the edges of the curtains. It was very early indeed. 'I had such a good night,' she mumbled, feeling the bed move as Hugo climbed from the other side. She'd never been so comfortable with someone so quickly. 'I'll get up and make you some breakfast before you go.'

His laugh was soft. 'That's okay, sleepyhead. Go back to sleep, I'm going to dress and rush away, there's no point in you getting up.'

'If you're sure,' she said, teetering on the edge of sleep.

'Positive.'

He kissed her again, a soft press of his lips against her cheek that made her smile and slip back into a contented, satisfied sleep.

It was the sound of the front door that woke her. In the winter, the wooden door became swollen and difficult to close, and it was impossible to do it quietly. She should have warned

Hugo. With a lazy stretch, her mind drifted back to the previous night. He'd been an attentive lover; it was a shame he'd had to rush away. It would have been pleasant to have stayed all morning getting to know one another better, making love again… and again.

When she opened her eyes, confused to see it was now almost bright, she reached for her mobile and flopped back against the pillow with it in her hand. Eight o'clock. Much later than she'd thought.

It was tempting to forget about going to Edgware, unsure after all if she should go to see Eric Thomas. She hadn't felt so good, so at ease… so satisfied… for a long time, it seemed such a shame to spoil it. But even the thought of Eric was enough to dampen her mood. The years hadn't dimmed the guilt she felt over what she'd done; she doubted if it had dimmed the anger that had emanated from Eric in waves when she'd seen him last almost twenty-five years before. With a moan, she rolled over and buried her head in the pillow. No, even if Hugo had wanted to linger, she'd have had to put him off, this mystery needed to be sorted. She needed to confront whoever was sending those emails. If it was Eric, she could stop him, somehow. She had to; she wanted to get on with her life, especially since she now had someone special to share it with.

Climbing from the bed, she slipped on a robe and went to open the curtains. It was a dull, cloudy day, the remnants of frost lingering on the roof tiles opposite telling her she needed to dress warmly. She turned back to look at the bed with a sigh but her satisfied smile dimmed when her eyes landed on something on the floor. In disbelief, she stepped closer. A used condom. He'd left it there. Disgust swept over her and she hurried into the en suite to pull toilet paper off the roll. She gathered the offending item and threw it into the waste basket. Later, she'd empty it into the bin outside.

Was she wrong to feel slightly demeaned by his carelessness or was she making too big a deal of it? It was an action that seemed so at odds with the sophisticated, charming man he was. She tried to brush it off as she showered and dressed in jeans and jumper. A slice of toast and a coffee and she was ready to deal with whatever else the day had to throw at her. The condom issue... she'd be brave and discuss that with Hugo the next time. Maybe a waste basket on his side of the bed was the answer. The prosaic thought almost made her smile and she tried to regain the euphoria she'd felt earlier.

But she didn't have a chance; all she could think of now was her meeting with Eric.

She pulled on a warm navy jacket, shoved her purse in one of its big pockets and left the apartment. The streets were Saturday morning quiet, the temperature chilly enough to keep her hands buried in her pockets as she walked briskly to Parsons Green station. She's already checked the best route and went to the correct platform to catch the District line to Embankment Station where she changed to the Northern Line. There were no delays and she arrived in Edgware a little over an hour later.

It was an area she'd never been to before but she'd inputted the address into her phone and looking at the directions as she exited the station, she was pleased to see it wasn't far. Ten minutes later, she was standing outside the huge glass-fronted showroom. There were several people milling around inside but none bore any resemblance to the gangly young man she remembered or the more up-to-date photo of Eric she'd seen on Cherry's Facebook page. There was no point in standing there, peering through the window, hoping for inspiration, so without further ado she stepped up to the front door. It was automatic and swished open in front of her, inviting her to come inside and look at the glossy cars displayed on shiny tiled floors. Her footsteps echoed strangely as if announcing her arrival but nobody came to greet her.

She walked slowly, fingers lingering on the paintwork of the cars as she passed, her eyes moving from person to person, seeking out the one she wanted to see. But there was no sign of him. Finally, a smiling woman, hair streaked in bright pink, appeared at her side. 'Can I help you?'

Melanie must have given a good impression of someone who was interested in buying, there was a hopeful look in the woman's eyes that faded as soon as Melanie spoke. 'Actually, I was looking for Eric Thomas. He's an old friend,' she added hastily as she saw the woman's eyebrows rise.

'He's on a tea break.' A hand with pink manicured nails pointed towards a seating area. 'If you want to wait, he'll be out in a few minutes.' The woman's eyes softened as she assessed Melanie and in a gentler tone added, 'I can go and get him if you like?'

'No, that's fine, I'll wait.' There were newspapers to while away the time, Melanie picked one up and was glancing through it when she saw Eric appear through a doorway on the far side of the showroom.

She wasn't expecting to see the young man of her childhood, but neither was she expecting the rather worn greying man with a protruding belly who ambled across the floor. The Facebook photograph, she guessed, was a few years out of date. He wasn't looking her way so she guessed the pink-haired woman hadn't told him about her. She was glad, she was able to observe him unnoticed and adjust her expectation to fit the reality.

Eric walked to a desk, sat down and immediately tapped keys on a keyboard as if picking up exactly where he'd left off before going on his break.

Melanie watched him for several seconds before getting to her feet. It was time to do what she'd gone there for. She crossed the showroom, but he didn't look up as she approached despite the loud slap of her leather soles on the tiled floor. It wasn't until she'd taken the seat on the other side of the desk that he looked up curiously, his fingers freezing as he stared at her.

'Hello, Eric,' she said, her voice trembling slightly. 'Remember me?'

The intense stare she remembered had gone, now his eyes were hooded, his mouth a thin slash in a pale face. His expression didn't seem to change as he looked at her. Surely, he remembered her. She'd not changed that much. Even if he didn't, she felt pinned to her seat by their shared history. Clearing her throat, she was about to tell him who she was when he held a hand up to stop her.

'I'm finished in an hour,' he said, without looking at her. 'There's a pub across the road, The Londoner, meet me there.' His fingers tapped again, quicker and quicker, then they stopped. 'Go,' he said, his lips barely moving.

Scrambling to her feet, she hurried across the showroom, almost losing her footing on the slippery floor, reaching the door and taking a deep breath as it swished open. Outside, she stood a moment in the chill breeze that edged around the building and tried not to cry. She should go home. This had been a crazy idea. Crazy.

She looked across the busy road towards the pub he'd mentioned. It was a grim-looking establishment, its original creamy brick streaked black from exhaust fumes, tiny windows like mean eyes looking across at her.

A crazy idea – but the only one she had.

Darting between the traffic, she crossed the road and pushed open the door of The Londoner. Inside, it was a pleasant surprise. White walls and clever lighting made it bright; chairs looked comfortable and tables were clean. A sign over the bar informed customers that breakfast was served all day and the pub was busy, crowded with people eating and filled with the loud noise of people chattering and laughing. She saw one small empty table at the back wall and negotiated her way around chairs and extended legs to get to it. There wasn't a vacant chair to be seen. She settled for a small stool; it was too small, too low but at least she could sit.

Propping her elbows on the table, she rested her chin on her joined hands and tried to let the surrounding din fill her head and drive out everything else. It was partially successful, the clashing orchestra of conversations forming a strange lullaby. As the lunchtime crowd thinned, tables became vacant and she moved from the stool to a chair at a table beside a small window. It overlooked the front of the pub and straight across the road to the car showroom. The hour was almost up; she fixed her eyes on the door until she saw Eric come out.

He'd ambled across the showroom floor earlier, but now he strode with a strange rolling gait, his face set and grim, hands tightened into fists at his side. He hadn't aged well. Only a year or so separated them but she would have guessed ten.

She was trembling by the time he came through the door and glared around the now half-empty pub. When his eyes lit on her, he stopped in his tracks and stared, then with a shake of his head he headed to the bar where he ordered a pint, downing half before turning and making his way to the table. He sat in the chair opposite without looking at her, put his drink on the table, leaned back and crossed his arms.

'You do remember me?' It was an unnecessary question. Only someone who knew exactly who she was and what she had done could look at her with such hatred.

It wasn't until he had picked up his pint and taken another mouthful that he answered, his lips twisted into a sneer.

'Remember you? How could I forget you? Anne Edwards, the woman responsible for my brother's death.'

12

Melanie hadn't been called by that name in so long it sounded strange to her ears, as if it referred to a different person. It did really, a much younger woman, a girl who'd made a silly mistake that had had terrible repercussions.

'I don't go by that name anymore. I use my mother's maiden name, Scott, and my middle name, Melanie.' By his expression, she guessed he already knew. He'd probably kept an eye on her over the years the same way she'd kept one on him. She couldn't argue with what he'd said. Not really. After all, she had been responsible for his brother Matthew's death.

She'd been fifteen, not a child, not yet a woman. Full of angst and hormones that raged even stronger when a new family had moved into the area and Matthew Thomas had joined her class. He was handsome, blue-eyed, blond-haired, a young Robert Redford, and her knees had turned to jelly when she was anywhere near him. She'd made it obvious, blushing scarlet when he spoke to her and looking at him in a doe-eyed way.

Children can be cruel, especially in packs. Melanie, delayed after school, had come out to find a gang of boys hanging around by the exit. She'd shot a shy smile at them; perhaps her eyes had lingered a bit too long on Matthew, perhaps she'd even fluttered her eyelashes. Whatever she'd done, the reaction was swift; Matthew was pushed and jostled with suggestions that she was up for it and he should go after her.

Mortified, Melanie had scurried away but not before she'd heard her handsome blue-eyed boy reply to their taunts in cruel, biting words. 'She's only a stupid little girl with no breasts and rabbit teeth, why would I be interested in her?'

Catcalls and jeers from the others followed her down the street as her young and very foolish heart broke. She ran from them as fast as she could, from their taunting laughter and vicious words, tears turning to sobs long before she arrived at her friend's house.

It was several minutes before she was calm enough to tell Cherry what had happened and by then anger had burst through her devastation, so she'd painted Matthew as the leader, the tormentor in chief.

Cherry had put an arm around her shoulders and told her what she should do. 'Get revenge,' she'd said, 'it will make you feel so much better.'

It had been Cherry who'd come up with the idea to start rumours about Matthew and it had been she who'd come up with exactly what to say. But it had been the foolish Anne Edwards who had immediately gone out and put the plan into action. She whispered to a friend that Matthew's family had been forced to move because he had molested a girl in his last school. She whispered to another that he'd given some girls an STD with no idea of what that meant, relying on Cherry's knowledge that it was something bad. And, because it was a small town and long ago, she told yet another that he was homosexual.

If she'd waited until the next day when the heat of her anger and the pain of rejection had worn off, she'd never have listened to her friend. She woke horrified at what she'd done and hurried to school to find the three friends and tell them she'd been joking. But her change of heart had come too late. Outside the school, a different friend approached her, eyes wide as she held her lips close to Melanie's ear and whispered, 'You'll never guess what I heard about Matthew Thomas!'

As one whispered to another, within days the rumours had spread everywhere, and by the end of the week Matthew Thomas was a pariah. His new classmates avoided him, stopped talking when he joined them, whispered loudly behind his back. There was suddenly no place for him on the school rugby team; nobody wanted to partner up with him for class projects or sit with him for lunch. In the second week, he stayed away from school.

A week later he was dead.

They were told at the school assembly, rows of students staring up at the podium where the principal stood looking pale and drawn, his words deliberately vague as he told them that one of their classmates had sadly passed away. But it was too small a town to hide the truth, and students who went home for lunch came back with the news that Matthew had drowned.

Melanie, who stayed in school for lunch, was in the corridor outside a classroom when Cherry hurried over to tell her the news. 'Matthew,' she said, grasping Melanie's arm. 'He killed himself, he jumped into the river.'

The words seemed to float on a chorus of sound whooshing around Melanie's head, the edges of her vision darkening until it was gone. When she came to, she was in the principal's office on a cold leather chaise longue and there were other voices floating

– this time above her head, loud condemnatory words in her mother's shrill voice.

'School should have been closed to allow family to have told the children in the comfort and security of their homes,' Mrs Edwards was saying.

The principal's voice was calm and reasonable. 'As I've said, Mrs Edwards, we didn't hear until a few minutes before assembly. It was too late at that point. We did envisage that some of the pupils might have heard during lunch and we had, in fact, organised counsellors to attend the school this afternoon. They're here now and if your daughter is feeling up to it, perhaps she should go back and listen to what they have to say.'

Melanie didn't want to do any such thing. What she wanted to do was scurry away and hide her guilt and shame.

Instead, her mother took her by the arm, with a grip that said she wasn't listening to any argument and led her back to her classroom. 'I'll wait,' she said, opening the door and giving Melanie a none-too-gentle push into the room.

Those who had whispered the rumours sat with tear-streaked, pinched faces. Not everyone knew she'd been the source of them, but the few who did turned towards her with accusing, condemning eyes. Soon, she guessed, taking her seat, they'd all know.

Melanie looked across the table at Eric. 'I never meant to hurt him.' The words were an echo from the past – the same words she'd said all those years ago when the police had come knocking on their door, a disgrace her embarrassed mother had never forgiven her for. 'I was a stupid, thoughtless child. He'd hurt me, I wanted to hurt him back.'

'Well, you succeeded, didn't you?' Eric drained his pint and without asking if she wanted anything, headed back to the bar.

Melanie watched his rigid back. Eric had been a year older than Matthew. She remembered him coming to their house and shouting at her, telling her that she'd murdered his brother as sure as if she'd held his head under the water. He'd not been the only one to point a finger of blame, but he'd been the most vocal. His parents had been stunned and shocked by the death of their youngest son. They'd never said a word to her but she remembered once, a day or two before she and her mother had left Wethersham, she'd seen them in the town and had wanted to say something, to apologise for her part in their son's death. But they'd crossed to the other side of the road and kept their faces averted as they passed her, as if she'd been something evil to avoid.

Eric returned, this time with a whisky chaser to accompany his pint. He stared into his drink for a few seconds before speaking in a low monotone she had to lean forward to hear. 'Matthew was really nervous starting the new school. The one he'd been to before was an all-boys one and he wasn't used to being with girls. He was a good-looking boy but clumsy and tongue-tied around them, never sure what to say.' Eric lifted his eyes and met hers across the table. 'He was the gentlest lad, you know, he'd never have meant to hurt you.'

Melanie swallowed convulsively and snuffled. She'd sobbed for his loss then, now she wanted to howl for him, for her, for the guilt that never faded.

Eric picked up his pint. He drank deeply, then stared into the glass. 'It was our parents' idea that Matthew stay off school for a while. They thought it was the right decision. That all the gossip would die down. Instead, it isolated him even more, drove him into himself. The day before... it happened... Matthew begged them to return to Leeds.' Eric looked up from his drink, his angry, sad eyes meeting hers. 'My father told him not to be stupid, that they weren't going to move again. When they found Matthew's body, he cried and begged for forgiveness but he never forgave himself, and neither did my mother. Matthew's suicide sentenced them to a life of bitter recriminations.'

Melanie felt the extra weight of guilt press her down. 'What I did was so cruel. I knew almost immediately and tried to stop it but it was too late. The tiny whispers kept growing.'

'Tell me,' Eric said, 'why did you never tell people it had been Cherry's idea?'

Melanie was surprised by the question. 'It was a difficult time. It might have been her idea, but I'm the one who actually started the rumours, not her.' She waited a beat, then asked, 'How did you know it had been her idea?'

Draining his pint, he put the empty glass down. 'It was obvious; you were the quiet, easily-led, mousey type, she was the troublesome shit-stirrer.' He picked up his whisky and emptied it in one mouthful. 'Now, whereas this has been a delightful walk down memory lane, I guess you had a reason for coming to see me.'

'Yes,' she said quietly. She curled in on herself, lowering her chin and folding her arms across her chest in a tight hug. 'Cherry is dead.' Melanie hadn't come to terms with the knowledge and there was a note of disbelief in the three barely audible words. Feeling Eric's eyes on her, she cleared her throat and looked up. 'Cherry, she's dead.'

'Dead?' He looked away, picked up his empty glass, then put it down with a grunt of frustration and rocked it backwards and forwards on the table. The sound of glass on wood was loud in the silence between them, a sad toll for a dead woman.

Melanie waited for him to say something more. When he didn't, she said, 'Yes, she's dead. Someone started rumours that destroyed her. I think it's the same person who has been sending me emails, taunting me about being Anne Edwards, trying to do the same to me.'

He laughed but there was no humour in the sound. 'And you think that might be me?'

'Is it?'

His face creased in a sneer. 'No, I've not sent you any damn emails.'

If his eyes were the windows to his soul, they were so hooded Melanie couldn't tell if he was lying or not. But if it wasn't him, who? 'Someone is sending them,' she said. 'Is there anyone you can think of who would do such a thing? Someone back then who made threats maybe?'

'You're talking twenty-five years ago, Anne. Everyone hated you then. Now' – he shrugged – 'people move on. I doubt if anyone gives the likes of you a second thought.'

She bristled at the sneer in his voice and the insult in his words. With an indrawn breath, she put some steel in her words. 'Someone set Cherry up, and someone is sending me emails. I'm going to find out who that is. If it isn't you, then you've nothing to worry about.'

'Then I've nothing to worry about,' he said, standing abruptly. 'I've wasted enough of my time; I only came to meet you out of curiosity. To see what kind of woman you grew into.' His eyes raked her. 'Now I know.'

'Well, in case you get enlightenment,' she said, reaching into her pocket for her purse and taking out a business card. 'Here's my card.' She quickly scribbled her mobile number across the bottom of it and held it out. 'Email or mobile number, you can contact me however you like.' She thought he'd ignore it, instead he snatched it from her hand without a word and left.

She peered out the window, watching as his long strides ate up the path. His final words had no power to hurt her, they were never destined to be friends. But she'd pinned her hopes on getting some information from him. Now, she was no better off.

The walk back to the station seemed longer or was it the hopelessness that made the journey seem unending. The train was busy but she managed to get a seat and pulled out her phone, hoping for a message from Hugo to brighten what had become a dull, depressing day. But there was nothing. There was an old-fashioned streak in her that said she should wait for him to contact her, that she shouldn't seem too keen. *Too desperate.* Oh, for goodness' sake, it was the twenty-first century, there was no shame in being first. Before she could change her mind, she tapped out a short text. *Thanks for a lovely evening and a wonderful night.*

Back at home, she made herself a cup of tea and took it through to the lounge. Her phone sat silently on the seat beside her; no answer from Hugo, no further emails from *nobody*.

With a sigh, she reached for the handle of her briefcase, grunting with annoyance when it tipped over and her laptop and the sheaf of reports slid out onto the carpet. She put her tea down on a side table, stooped to pick up her laptop and put it on the sofa. Luckily, although the reports had fanned out, they'd stayed in order. She shuffled them into a neat pile, picked it up and sat back with it on her lap.

Within minutes, she was lost in the details of the merger, sipping her tea as she read, satisfied as everything made perfect sense. Things were proceeding as they'd planned. She noted dates of future meetings and opened her laptop to check they were all in her diary. Checking and double-checking, leaving nothing to chance. It was the way she worked; it was why she was good at what she did.

It was late afternoon by the time she finished. Her phone was still sitting silently beside her. Hugo had said he'd be in touch later but he hadn't specified a time. He'd ring soon and maybe they'd go out for dinner or a drink... something. Something. She shivered at the thought. The sex had been amazing; he'd been a skilled and generous lover. She picked up the phone, read the message she'd sent and smiled, it was unexceptional. He was probably busy in meetings or something; when he was free, he'd read it and reply.

The smile lingered as she thought about him. He was what her life needed to make it complete. A woman she'd worked with years before had called the man she'd been dating a *keeper*, an expression Melanie hadn't heard before. Now, she understood it completely. Hugo, she decided was definitely a *keeper*.

She would have preferred to have kept her thoughts on him but as the light faded and shadows filled the room, they drifted to Eric Thomas and she heaved a sad sigh. She shouldn't have been surprised at the extent of his anger and hatred, after all, her guilt hadn't faded with the years. Strangely enough, despite his animosity, she believed him when he said he'd had nothing to do with the emails. She'd wanted it to have been him; he had a reason to hate her. It was a disturbing thought to think that someone else hated her so much.

She switched on the TV to watch the six o'clock news, keeping the volume low and her phone close by. Hugo was sure to ring soon.

By eight, her belief had wavered, and by ten it had faded completely.

13

Melanie slept badly, waking frequently with the certainty that her phone was ringing. Every time, she'd switch on the light and reach for it, prepared to be effusively forgiving at Hugo calling so late. Each time the blank phone told her she'd been dreaming.

Maybe he'd been in an accident and was lying injured in a hospital somewhere. By morning, she was convinced something must have happened to him. She went through to the lounge and switched on the TV, expecting to hear news about some atrocity that he might have been embroiled in. When there was nothing, she switched on her laptop and spent an hour fruitlessly searching for any reason to excuse him and finding nothing remotely plausible.

Doubts slithered into her head, curled around her brain and squeezed. Had she made a mess of it? Was that it? Perhaps she'd said something wrong or he'd found her cold and unadventurous in bed. Had she been found wanting?

Back in bed, she tried to get some sleep but images of Hugo and Eric danced beneath her eyelids, one tantalising, the other taunting, both disturbing. With a groan, she threw back her duvet and swung her feet to the floor. She was supposed to be meeting her friend Caitlin for lunch to make up for abandoning their plans the previous week; Melanie would have a long shower and see if she felt up to it.

~

An hour later, showered and dressed, she didn't feel much better. It would be unfair to cancel lunch again, but maybe she could change their plans. It was eleven; Caitlin was sure to be awake. Melanie picked up her mobile, checked again for any messages and rang her number, holding the phone away from her ear when her friend almost shrieked down the phone.

'Melanie! I want to hear about your date with Mr Charming.'

'I'll tell you everything, but I didn't sleep well, would you settle for coffee here rather than going for lunch?'

'Perfect, as long as you give me all the details. I'll be there in an hour.'

Melanie hung up and smiled. Her friend's company was the tonic she needed. She had met Caitlin Ballantyne at a 'Law and Order in the Twenty-First Century' conference they'd attended five months earlier. The final talk of the day had been stultifyingly boring and after it, the woman sitting on the seat beside her had nudged her and rolled her eyes. 'Hell's bells, that was boring. I need a drink, you coming?'

They'd absconded to the hotel bar where they'd spent the next couple of hours drinking G&Ts, chatting and discovering that they'd much in common. Both were heading for the top in careers still very male-dominated, Melanie as a corporate lawyer, Caitlin as a newly-appointed detective inspector with the Metropolitan Police. They'd quickly become friends, falling into regular meetings, sometimes after work for dinner or drinks, occasionally for lunch.

~

Caitlin was a woman of her word and almost on the dot of sixty minutes later, Melanie smiled to hear the doorbell ring and hurried to open the door.

'I want to hear everything.' Caitlin followed her back into the kitchen, threw her coat on a chair and slumped onto another, stretching out her long legs with a sigh. 'And no leaving bits out. I'm a detective, I'll spot the gaps.'

Melanie poured coffee, then sat opposite and told her friend about the dinner on Friday night and how it had been so pleasant, so easy. 'He's so interesting and interested in what I have to say too. It was one of the best nights I've had in a while.' She sipped her coffee, her fingers linked around the mug. 'Afterwards, he drove me home.'

Caitlin gave a dirty laugh. 'Oh ho, we're getting to the good bit.'

Melanie shot her a look. How old was she? Five? Suddenly, she regretted inviting her, she could have made up an excuse, said she was tired – which would have been true.

'Was he good?'

There was no point in lying, in saying Hugo had dropped her at the door and gone away. Caitlin wasn't kidding when she said she'd spot the gaps. Melanie often wondered how she managed to keep anything from her. 'Yes,' she admitted. 'It was simply magical.' She hesitated before giving a dismissive shrug. 'He left early yesterday morning, said he'd ring me later, but...' Her voice trailed off and she dropped her gaze to the table.

'You haven't heard from him?'

Melanie shook her head. 'I had a meeting, when it was over

and I hadn't heard from him, I sent him a message saying how much I enjoyed the night.' She reached for her phone, looked at it and pushed it across the table. 'See.'

Caitlin looked at the phone and a frown creased her brow. 'A bit odd that he hasn't replied, but maybe he's busy. Maybe he meant to say he'd ring you later in the week.'

'He said *later*, in anyone's book that means the same day,' Melanie said, refusing to take the crutch she'd been offered. She wasn't going to spend the rest of the week wondering if Hugo was going to phone.

'Yes, you're right, it does. You said he had a website, can I see it.'

'Not sure why you'd want to,' Melanie said grumpily but she got to her feet and went for her laptop. She set it on the table between them and switched it on. 'It doesn't say much about him,' she warned as her fingers flew over the keys. 'It shows the kind of work he's involved in. Plus, there's a photo of him.'

Caitlin reached for the coffee pot and refilled both their mugs. 'What's keeping you?' she asked, picking up her coffee.

'I can't find it,' Melanie said, pressing a few more keys. 'Very odd, it should have popped up when I put in his name.' Concentrating, she tapped out his name again, then looked up to meet Caitlin's concerned gaze. 'He's not here.' She didn't resist when her friend pulled the computer away.

'Hugo Field, you said.'

Melanie murmured *yes*. There was a heavy, numb weight where her heart was supposed to be. She watched Caitlin's fingers move over the keyboard, strangely surprised to see she was an advocate of the two-finger tapping method, she'd have assumed more expertise. Melanie's mind was darting anywhere, everywhere rather than facing the truth, but she had to when Caitlin looked over, her face a mask of concern, her eyes soft with pity.

'I've been ghosted, haven't I?' Melanie had read about it, pitying the poor fools who had been the victim of a sleazy person who suddenly and without warning stopped communicating, vanishing from social media, never to be heard from again. It was something that happened to other people. Not to her.

'It certainly looks like ghosting,' Caitlin said, shutting the laptop. 'A website that vanishes, your message not read. Have you tried ringing his number?'

Melanie hadn't. She picked up her phone and rang it, putting it down seconds later. 'Surprise, surprise, the number is no longer in service.' She saw Caitlin's sympathetic expression and battled to make her own appear unconcerned.

She obviously wasn't a successful actor. Caitlin reached across and grabbed her arm. 'Oh Mel, I'm so sorry. What a bastard.'

'It's a new experience for me. I should have guessed it was all too good to be true.' Melanie pushed away from the table and got to her feet. 'More coffee?'

Caitlin shook her head but Melanie moved across to the kitchen and filled the kettle to make more, needing to be doing something.

'Some guys like to play games,' Caitlin said. 'He is probably a low-achiever who gets his kicks from pretending to be something he's not to attract professional women who probably wouldn't normally have looked twice at him.'

Melanie was about to say she didn't care what he worked at but stopped herself. Hadn't she been impressed when Hugo had said he was an architect and, although art wasn't her thing, hadn't she been a little impressed by his intelligent conversation? She wondered how much of what Caitlin said was true. 'He was older than me, Caitlin, maybe fifty. I thought we were both past the age of playing games.' Melanie rubbed her eyes to dislodge a gathering tear. 'I thought too, that I had much better judgement.' She filled her mug with coffee and picked it up. 'Let's sit in the lounge, it'll be more comfortable.' The sun was streaming into the room but it didn't brighten her mood. She sat on the sofa, kicked off her shoes and rested the warm mug against her chest, trying to thaw the ice that had lodged there. 'What a shit he is,' she said. She heard the trace of bitterness that had crept into her voice and hated the man even more. 'I'd guess his name isn't Hugo Field either.'

'Probably not,' Caitlin said, sitting beside her.

There was silence for several minutes. Melanie sipped her coffee and tried to remember every word of each conversation she'd had with Hugo. How many lies had he told her? Had she amused him with her gullibility? Her thoughts were interrupted by Caitlin's puzzled, 'Where did that come from?'

'What?'

'That.' Caitlin pointed to the bookshelf opposite. She stood and went over to pick up the frame that had caught her attention.

Colour flushed Melanie's cheeks. 'You brought the police magazine to show me the article they'd written about you last month, remember? You left it here. I asked if you wanted it back and you told me to dump it.' She waved a hand at the frame in Caitlin's hand. 'It was such a good photo of you, I thought I'd keep it. I had a spare frame and it fit...' Her voice tailed away. 'I didn't think you'd mind.'

'Of course, I don't mind, silly.' Caitlin gave a quick laugh. 'I'm flattered. Surprised to see it, I suppose, especially with my rank blazoned across the end of it. Makes me sound so important, *Detective Inspector Ballantyne.*' Replacing the frame carefully in the same spot on the shelf, she turned with an embarrassed grin. 'Sorry, I suppose I'm still not used to having succeeded, a bit like you being made partner.'

'Yes,' Melanie said, feeling her shoulders droop. Success in her work, that should be enough.

'You know,' Caitlin said, waving her mug, 'I think you need a glass of wine to drown this crappy day rather than coffee. Do you have any?'

'There's half a bottle in the fridge. I've been meaning to buy more.'

'Half a bottle isn't going to do it, my friend. I'll pop out to the supermarket and get some wine and food. It'll take me thirty minutes, why don't you try to get some sleep.' She held out her hand. 'Give me your keys, I'll let myself in and if you're asleep, I'll drink wine until you wake.'

It sounded like a good plan and Melanie was happy to let her friend take over, handing her the house keys and sinking back onto the sofa as Caitlin pulled on her coat.

'Okay, shut your eyes, and get some sleep. I'll be back in a while.'

'Yes, mother.' Melanie smiled and closed her tired eyes. She listened as her friend's footsteps crossed the hall to the front door and the scrape and clunk as the door shut, then to her surprise she did fall asleep.

It was the ache in her neck from the awkward angle her head was in that woke her. Sitting up, she stretched and rotated her shoulders, giving a squeal of fright to see Caitlin staring at her from a chair near the French window. 'Bloody hell,' Melanie said, 'how long have you been sitting there?'

Caitlin held up her glass. 'About two mouthfuls. You were out for the count.' She pointed to the table beside the sofa where the wine bottle and a glass were waiting. 'Help yourself.'

Melanie hadn't eaten since the day before. She couldn't

afford to go to work stinking of booze again. Pouring a small amount into the glass, she sat back. 'Here's to us.'

'Here's to surviving all the crap that life throws at us.'

'To surviving,' Melanie said, leaning forward and reaching out to touch her glass to her friend's. She wished she could tell Caitlin about the other problem she had. But she couldn't. Caitlin didn't know about Anne Edwards. Melanie wanted to keep it that way, wanted to keep this life free from the taint of her past.

They finished the bottle of wine and ate supermarket lasagne as they swopped stories of ghastly men they'd met and their strange peccadillos, giggling over the worst lovers they'd had, smiling over the best and the ones they regretted letting go. It was the perfect funeral for Hugo Field. Instead of self-pity, Melanie felt the stirrings of healthy anger. *Hugo Field, what a shit.*

It was nearly nine before Caitlin looked at her watch. 'I'd better go. You sure you're okay?' She pulled Melanie into a hug. 'I can stay over if you like.'

'No, honestly, I'm fine. I'm over the first shock.' She pulled back and met her friend's steady gaze. 'In a few days it'll be a bad memory and I'll be saying *Hugo who*?' Arm in arm they walked to the front door where with a final hug, Caitlin left.

Melanie stood and watched as her friend walked down the street, then stepped back into the silence of her apartment. She pushed the door shut, reminded suddenly of Hugo's exit the morning before when she was still dreaming of happy ever after. *Hugo who*. Brave words. How stupid she'd been to build a dream on a puff of smoke. Perhaps she should have asked Caitlin to stay over but she guessed that would have been putting off the inevitability of facing the loneliness of her life.

Back in the lounge, she was unable to resist the temptation and picked up her phone to check for messages, a soft sigh escaping when there was none. At least there were no further emails from *nobody*. Perhaps, despite his denial, it had been Eric Thomas who'd been responsible for them and her visit had frightened him away. Maybe he'd seen she wasn't the stupid little girl she'd been all those years before.

Maybe.

14

Despite all the conflicting thoughts running through her head, Melanie slept well and headed to the office in a far calmer frame of mind. The day passed in a blur of meetings, of reports received and sent, and organisational decisions that came easily. When Caitlin rang Melanie's office during the afternoon to ask how she was, she was able to tell her with honesty that she was feeling much better. 'My head is going *Hugo who* now,' she said with a short laugh to cover the lie in the words. It would take more than a few days for the disappointment to fade and the hurt to heal but her friend didn't need to know that. She promised to meet her for a drink later in the week and hung up.

By the end of the week, all she was left with was a faint trace of regret. After all, nothing had been harmed apart from her pride. It helped that it had been a good week. There had been no further emails from *nobody* and the merger was galloping along without the slightest hiccup.

The week, however, wasn't over yet.

When her office phone rang mid-morning on Friday, she wasn't expecting any surprises.

'I need to see you,' the voice said without any introduction. It didn't need one, Richard Masters' voice was sufficiently distinctive.

'Certainly,' she said. 'When would–'

'Immediately,' he interrupted and hung up without another word.

Melanie frowned and quickly thought over the recent reports and meetings. There'd been nothing untoward. She slipped on her jacket, smoothed a hand over her hair, and headed upstairs.

From the urgency in his voice she'd expected to find Richard's office filled with other junior partners and her heart sank when she realised she was the only one. She'd made an error somewhere, and by the look of Richard's stern expression it was a serious one.

'Sit down,' he said.

She took some comfort from his pleasant tone of voice. She'd heard him angry and was glad that wasn't being directed her way. With the idea that action was better than passivity, she asked, 'Is there a problem?'

He rested his elbows on the desk, joined his long bony fingers at the tips and tapped them together rhythmically. 'Is there a problem,' he repeated her words, his deep voice making them sound more ominous. 'You tell me.'

Games... why did people want to play games? Hugo Field's handsome face came looming into her head, causing her to lift her chin and glare across the vast expanse of desk. 'As far as I am aware, Richard, there are no problems so if there is something on your mind, I would appreciate you spitting it out.'

Richard seemed briefly taken aback by her sharp tone and the finger tapping ceased abruptly. 'Fair enough,' he said but there was still no hint of anger in his voice. 'I don't have to tell you, Melanie, how delicate the negotiations regarding this Fanton's-CityEast merger are.' He clasped his fingers together and dropped his hands to the desk.

The thump was loud, disconcerting – intimidating. Melanie kept her chin in the air and said nothing.

'It seems we may have a leak somewhere.' The words hung between them in a silence that lasted several seconds.

Melanie didn't react, trying to absorb what this meant... what it meant for her.

'You understand what I'm saying,' he said, a level of irritation creeping into his voice.

Of course, she understood. Secrecy in these negotiations was of vital importance; everyone knew that, confidentiality was one of the linchpins of Masters Corporate Law. 'Yes, I understand,' she said finally. 'Have there been rumours?'

Richard sat back and crossed his arms. 'Worse, I'm afraid. There has been some unusual activity in the stock market. Someone has been buying up CityEast shares.'

Melanie shut her eyes briefly. When the merger went through, those shares would be worth double, maybe triple their current value. Insider trading... it was illegal but a huge temptation for someone with knowledge of the future.

'It was none of our staff,' Melanie said. 'Maybe someone in either Fanton's or CityEast?'

'I've had Deanne Sandler on to me this morning. She's not a happy lady.'

Melanie admired the CEO of CityEast. Deanne was smart, tough and had a reputation as someone who didn't suffer fools gladly. 'She's looking into her staff?'

'Yes, as is John Backhoe in Fanton's. Every email account is being checked, there's nowhere for the bastard to hide.'

Melanie heard the anger in Richard's voice now; it had probably been there all along simmering under the surface. Anger directed at whoever would dare try to damage Masters' reputation. Richard was right, of course, there was no place to hide. Whoever was responsible would be caught and hung up to dry.

Back in her office, she sat and stared at her laptop. Shocked as she was by the news, there was something else bothering her... something niggling. Her eyes swept around the room. What was it? Finally, her eyes rested on the briefcase she'd dropped onto a chair when she'd arrived that morning. She'd not opened it yet, and it sat there with its buckles tightly fastened. It had been the first thing she'd bought herself when she joined the firm; it had been expensive, the leather soft but strong, the two old-fashioned buckles finicky to open and close. She used it every day and it had got better, softer with the years. The only downside was that if you lifted it by the handle when the buckles weren't closed, things tended to fall out of it. As they had on Saturday morning.

But she hadn't opened it when she got home on Friday.

15

Melanie sat for almost an hour going over and over the sequence of events. She was certain she hadn't opened her briefcase when she got home on Friday, too excited about her date to want to do any work. *Her date.* There was the corrosive taste of bitterness on her tongue.

Hugo Field. She'd been used.

Her laptop had been inside her briefcase but it was password protected. That hadn't been her downfall. It was the reports she'd brought home to read: they were annotated with the meetings that had taken place or were planned with the CEOs of the two investment banks. It would be relatively easy for anyone to put two and two together. And she'd told him, hadn't she? Melanie swallowed the lump in her throat and pressed her lips together to stop them trembling. In the restaurant, over that romantic dinner when she had laughed and flirted and thought all her dreams had come true, she'd told him she'd brought reports home to read.

She dropped her forehead onto the palm of her hand and groaned. When he'd invited her to Slovakia, she'd told him the damn time frame for the deal when she told the bastard she'd be free in two weeks. When it got out – and it would – she'd be destroyed. All her years of work, all the long hours and sacrifice, all to end like this.

Even if she could convince the senior partners that she'd not done it for financial gain, her judgement would be called into question. Richard Masters would fire her and nobody else would take her on. She might even be debarred.

She looked around the tiny office she'd been so incredibly proud of, and felt the walls close in on her. Everyone would be disappointed and disgusted with her. There would be criticism of the senior partners for offering her the junior partnership, and Masters itself would be diminished as a result.

Her fingers gripped the edge of her desk. Maybe there was one thing she could do. She couldn't turn back the clock to that first meeting with Hugo and see him for the nasty conniving bastard he'd proved himself to be, but at least she could ensure he didn't gain from his deviousness. She would tell Richard, confess what she'd done. If she did it now, perhaps he'd have a chance to limit the damage.

Two minutes later, having impressed upon his PA the urgency of speaking to him, she was seated in the same chair she'd vacated so innocently over an hour before. 'It was my fault,' she said before he had a chance to ask why she was there. 'I'll tell you everything.'

Ten minutes later, she sat back with a dry mouth. She could tell nothing from Richard's expression. Even his long fingers, curled over the rounded arms of his chair, were still. 'Hugo Field,' he said, the two words growled out in his deep voice. He moved abruptly, startling a gasp from Melanie, and pulled over the keyboard of his desktop computer.

He wouldn't find anything. She could have told him but it seemed a better idea to let him find it out for himself.

Richard Masters wasn't a man who gave up easily so it was

almost five minutes later before he pushed the keyboard away with a grunt of irritation. 'Okay,' he said.

Melanie waited for the words she expected to hear. *You're fired. You're a disgrace to the profession. A disgrace to Masters.*

'Let's see if there's a way out of all of this.'

Her look of surprise must have been impressive. Richard Masters smiled. 'What? Did you think I was going to throw you to the wolves?'

'I've let you down, endangered the merger and the reputation of the company.'

'Yes, you've been an absolute idiot,' Masters agreed. 'But coming to me as soon as you realised the truth was exactly the right thing to do. And it took guts.' He smiled at her. 'Guts impress me.' He reached for his desk phone. 'Now let's ensure this Hugo Field gets what's coming to him.' Masters tapped out a number and sat back as it rang.

'I want to speak to Detective Inspector Sam Elliot,' he said when the phone was answered.

Shock seared Melanie. The police! She felt tension rise as Masters gave the details of what had happened including a brief précis of what she had told him about her dealings with Hugo Field.

'Fine, I'll tell her to go home. It would be better to meet her there. Her address is...' Masters raised an eyebrow at Melanie who obligingly reeled off her address.

Masters put the phone down. 'Don't look so worried,' he said to her. 'We've dealt with the City of London Police Fraud Team before. Sam Elliot is one of their best, we've worked with him a number of times.' He saw her look of surprise. 'I've been in this business a long time, Melanie, I could tell you tales that would make your eyes pop.' His expression tightened. 'Go home, talk to Sam. Give him whatever you can to help him catch this bastard. Meanwhile, I'm going to talk to people in CityEast and Fanton's.' He tapped a finger on the desk. 'I'd guess that your pal, Hugo, was hoping to make a quick killing. I think I can safely say that the merger has hit a complication and will be delayed, possibly by several months.'

That was one way to stop the bastard; inside traders tended to want a smash-and-grab-type of situation. 'If they do catch him, though, I won't be able to prove he opened my briefcase and took information.'

Masters screwed up his nose. 'Let's worry about that after we find him. I bet it isn't his first time to be involved in shady financial dealings.'

There was nothing further to be said except, 'Thank you. I will do whatever I can to make this better.'

Back in her office, she told Rona she had an appointment and wouldn't be available for the rest of the day. She put the phone down before she was asked any details, picked up her belongings and headed home.

She'd always loved her apartment but when she opened the front door and stepped into the hallway, all she could think of was Hugo and the night he had spent there. In the lounge, she looked at where she'd put her briefcase – the same place she put it every single day. She imagined Hugo opening it and rummaging through with his greedy conniving hands. How stupid she had been; she'd handed everything to him on a plate – the knowledge of the reports and time to help himself to their contents while she slept in a post-coital glow.

Anger surged through her but it had been replaced by a resigned sadness by the time the doorbell went. She opened the door to Detective Inspector Sam Elliot, a slim man with thinning brown hair, a pleasant, unremarkable face and kind eyes that instantly reassured Melanie.

Shutting the front door, she waved him into the lounge.

'Have a seat,' she said. 'Would you like some tea or coffee?'

'No, thank you, I'm good.' Elliot took off his jacket and hung it on the back of the chair before sitting. His white shirt was neat, his tie decidedly bizarre, luridly coloured and wildly patterned. He saw her looking, picked up the end of it and looked down before dropping it with a wide smile. 'My daughter bought it for my birthday. It's pretty hideous but...'

Suddenly, it didn't look so bad. 'You must love her very much,' she said, relaxing a little and taking a seat on the sofa.

'I do,' he said. 'Now why don't you tell me everything from the beginning.'

Fifteen minutes later, leaving nothing out, Melanie sat back with a sigh. 'That's it. That's the whole sad, embarrassing, career-wrecking saga.'

'Mr Masters didn't give me the impression that your career was any way in trouble.'

'I've only recently been promoted to junior partner, it comes with a three-month probation. What do you think my chances are?'

Elliot tilted his head and looked at her. 'I've known Richard Masters for some years. He's a very fair man. I think he'd appreciate the quick acknowledgment of your part in this.'

'He said he liked my guts in coming forward,' she admitted.

'There you go then. So, forget about that.'

She felt a slight release in the bands of tension that had gripped her since she'd realised what had happened. 'Okay, I'll try. So, what happens now?'

Elliot put his notebook away and ran a hand over his head. 'I appreciate you want to help and I'm grateful you've told me your story.' He leaned closer, his garish tie swinging forward. 'But I doubt very much if Hugo Field is this man's name so we have no way of identifying him. Chances are he's bought the shares through a variety of proxies. I'll search where I can, obviously, but I'm not holding my breath.'

'I see,' Melanie said. It all seemed to be a waste of time. 'I suppose it's too late to try to get fingerprints from my briefcase.'

'A bit,' Elliot said with a smile.

She frowned as a thought came to her. 'What about DNA? Could you find out who he was from that?'

It was Elliot's turn to frown. 'If he'd been convicted of a crime it might be in our system, yes but...' He held a hand up. 'I suppose I don't have to ask.' He reached behind him for his jacket, put his hand into the pocket and pulled out an evidence bag. 'Okay, here you go.'

Melanie took it and left the room. She had to remove a couple of cotton face pads out of the way before seeing what she wanted. Screwing up her nose, she opened the evidence bag, picked up the clump of toilet paper with its disgusting contents, dropped it inside and secured the top.

DI Elliot took it from her as if it were the kind of thing he was handed on a routine basis.

His calm acceptance made Melanie smile. 'Does nothing ever faze you?'

'Very little.' He stood, pulled on his jacket and put the evidence bag into his pocket. 'Would you come into the station and work with a police artist to give us a likeness of Hugo Field?'

'I don't need to–'

'The sooner we can identify him the better,' he said, interrupting her.

'No, I meant that I don't need to work with an artist. I have a photo of Hugo.' Reaching for her phone, she brought it up. 'I took a shot of the thumbnail photo on the website he had; I was planning to show Caitlin the handsome new man in my life.'

Melanie heard the edge of bitterness in her voice and sighed. 'Anyway, there he is.'

Elliot looked at it and gave a satisfied nod. 'Perfect,' he said, taking it from her, 'I'll send it to mine.' He handed her phone back and turned to leave, stopping to peer at her bookcase. 'I know her,' he said, picking up a photo frame. 'Caitlin Ballantyne.' He put it down and looked back to Melanie. 'A relative of yours?'

'A friend.'

'It's good to have friends.' Reaching into his top pocket, he took out a card and handed it to her. 'If you think of anything else, anything at all, give me a buzz.'

'You will find him, won't you?' she said, taking it.

'I'll do my best,' he said, and with a wave he was gone.

16

Melanie sat for a long time after he'd left. The prospect of the evening ahead obsessing over Hugo... what he had done and how he'd almost ruined her career... chilled her. She needed company. It wasn't hard to decide who; of her few friends, it was Caitlin who would understand most easily.

Melanie was in luck and the phone was answered on the second ring. 'I've had a shit day,' she said without preamble. 'Can you come over?'

'Have you any food in the house? I skipped breakfast and missed lunch so I could eat a scabby babe.'

Melanie was used to her friend's rather choice use of words. 'Not a lot of food, but I still have the rest of the wine you bought last time you were here. I'll order some food in. What would you like? Italian?' She'd have preferred Indian but Caitlin, she knew, wasn't that keen on spicy food.

'Perfect,' Caitlin agreed. Melanie scribbled down Caitlin's preferences and hung up. She checked her phone for the number of the local Italian restaurant and rang to order. While she waited, she went to her bedroom and changed into jersey pyjamas. Comfort food and comfort dressing. It was almost the perfect evening.

With a sigh, she put a bottle of white wine in the fridge and set the table.

~

Caitlin arrived before the food, all effusive greetings and loud, cheery comments. She took the glass of wine Melanie offered and they sat at the table.

'I needed this,' Caitlin said, taking a large gulp. 'I don't know how bad your day was but it couldn't possibly beat mine.'

'I think Hugo used information he stole from me to buy up shares in CityEast.'

Caitlin choked on her wine, coughing and spluttering, banging her hand on her chest. 'What?' she squawked as she continued to cough.

'There's been a run on shares, bad enough to have aroused suspicion. They suspected a leak somewhere but…' Melanie swallowed a mouthful of wine. 'I knew… almost immediately, I think, that it was him. He'd looked in my briefcase that night and got enough information from the notes I had there.'

'Insider trading,' Caitlin said, her voice back to normal. 'Gosh, I'm so sorry. Maybe they won't find out it was you, although it's so hard to hide these things nowadays.'

'You think I don't know that,' Melanie snapped.

Caitlin held her hands up. 'Whoa, I'm sorry. Listen, I know how hard you've worked, and for it to end like this is so tough.' She reached over and gripped Melanie's arm. 'Did they fire you outright or suspend you?'

The doorbell pealed. 'It's the food.' Melanie stood, grabbed her purse and went to answer the door. She arrived back seconds later with laden bags. 'I bought everything you asked for and a bit more,' she said, unpacking it on the countertop.

Caitlin moved closer and put an arm around her shoulder. 'You'll be okay,' she said quietly. 'You'll find something else, maybe not in law, but there are other jobs–'

'I haven't been fired or suspended.' Melanie handed her a plate. 'Here, get some food and I'll tell you everything that happened afterwards.'

'Afterwards?'

Melanie shook her head. It wasn't until they were sitting at the table that she told her friend about her meeting with Richard Masters and the subsequent visit by DI Elliot.

'Sam Elliot?' Caitlin asked through a mouthful of pasta. 'I know him, a well-regarded officer.'

'Good, because he needs to find Hugo then I'll be totally exonerated.'

'But Richard didn't even suspend you? That's amazing. Fantastic. You've been so lucky.'

'Lucky... yes.' Melanie sighed, put her fork down and pushed the plate away. Caitlin didn't know the half of it; didn't know about Wethersham or that she'd once been a stupid, thoughtless girl called Anne Edwards who had done something so shockingly dreadful that it had never been forgotten. Melanie stood abruptly. 'I need to go to the bathroom.'

When she came back a few minutes later, Caitlin had finished her glass of wine and was reaching for the bottle. 'You okay?'

'Yes, sorry, I'm fine.' Melanie sat and reached for her glass.

'You have a message.'

'What?' The word was dragged out of her, full of frustration and barely contained anger.

Caitlin stared at her. 'Chill. A message. Your phone pinged.'

Melanie looked across the room to where her phone sat on a

shelf. She desperately wanted to look at it. Crossing the room, she picked it up, keeping her expression carefully neutral.

'Something important?'

'Only spam,' Melanie said, dismissing it. With the phone in her hand, she came back to the table, picked up her glass and headed to the window. 'I thought I heard rain and I was right, it's chucking it down. You'd better get a taxi home.'

'Never mind the weather,' Caitlin said, 'what are you going to do now?'

'My job. The merger may be delayed but it'll still go through. It's more important than ever that the rest of it is smooth and trouble free. I owe it to Richard.'

'Yes, I think you do.' Caitlin sipped her wine. 'I'm really surprised. From what you'd told me about him, I wouldn't have expected him to be so reasonable. I would have thought he'd have flayed you alive.'

Melanie looked into the rain-washed darkness of the window and saw her friend's reflection. Distorted by rain, it looked for a moment as if she were sneering, her face screwed up and angry. She turned with an exclamation on her lips, to ask what she'd done, stopping in time when she saw Caitlin's expression as it always was, pleasant and open. She shut her eyes, and quickly turned back to the window. It was she who was twisted and screwed up, she who constantly made a mess of things. She wished she could confess to her friend that this business with Hugo and the shares weren't what was churning her gut and sending shivers down her spine. The merger would eventually go ahead, and Hugo would either be caught and punished, or what was more likely, disappear.

It is said that confession is good for the soul, but how could it be? She liked the version of herself that Caitlin knew. Melanie Scott not Anne Edwards. Telling her about it all, the emails, Cherry's suicide, and her part in Matthew Thomas's death would destroy everything she'd tried to make of herself, everything she was, everything she wanted to be.

Her mobile felt hot in her hand. She didn't need to look at it again to remember the email that had come. As with the others, it was short. The words, once read, were hard to forget.

Only three words. But with the power to terrify and to put everything else into second place.

Time to pay

17

Melanie shook her head when Caitlin offered to stay overnight. 'Thank you, but honestly I'll be fine.'

'If you're sure,' she said, giving Melanie a hug. 'Promise me you'll ring if you're the slightest bit worried or anxious. Or anything.' She gave her a sloppy kiss on the cheek. 'Even if you simply want some reassurance, ring, okay?'

'I promise.' Melanie pushed her out the door and walked to the gate with her when the taxi drew up outside.

'Okay, I'll ring you in the morning to check you're all right.' Caitlin gave her arm a final squeeze before climbing into the waiting taxi.

Melanie waited until it had pulled away, her hand raised in a wave that tried very hard to be casual, dropping as soon as the car was out of sight. It was late. Streetlights cast strange shadows that seemed to move in the soft breeze that blew. Did shadows normally move? Walking backwards to the front door, she almost tripped over the step, stumbling and righting herself without taking her eyes from the shapes that continued to flicker.

'Idiot,' she mumbled as she shut the door and slipped on the safety chain. They were merely shadows, nothing more. Nevertheless, she peeped through the bedroom shutters, her eyes sweeping up and down the street. She should have let Caitlin stay. One night, it wouldn't have done any harm.

Back in the lounge, Melanie switched out the lights and sat to look out over the garden, but suddenly there were too many shadows, too many dark corners where something might lurk. *Time to pay.* She jumped up and dragged the curtains across, holding them clasped in her hands as she rested her forehead against them. Then, from behind, she heard the ping of her phone. She wouldn't look. Couldn't look without falling apart.

Avoiding even a glimpse in its direction, she hurried from the room. The bedroom door didn't have a key. There was no logic in her action, but she dragged the chest of drawers across the door before scurrying under the duvet and pulling it over her head. She didn't sleep. In the dark cave of the bed, she was terror's hostage, her imagination interpreting the three words in evermore brutal and graphic ways, the images switching and flickering constantly, technicolour one minute, grainy black and white the next. It wasn't until light seeped around the edges of the duvet that she pushed it back, then exhausted, she slept for a while until a loud cry woke her. She sat up, startled, listening, sinking down again in the realisation it had been her voice, her cry. Her pain.

The distant sound of the house phone ringing made her sit up again. She rarely used it; most people rang her mobile. She frowned as it continued to ring, stopped, and seconds later rang again. 'Caitlin,' Melanie muttered, throwing the duvet back. She looked at the chest of drawers barring her exit, shaking her head at her stupidity as she pushed it out of the way. The phone continued to ring, stopping as she got to the lounge. Then it started again. She picked it up. 'Sorry, I was in the shower.' The lie came easily.

'You scared the wits out of me, you idiot.' Caitlin's voice was agitated. 'You didn't answer your mobile, I was giving your house phone one more go before I rang the police.' A deep, noisy exhale of breath. 'You scared me, Mel,' she said, her voice calmer. 'How are you this morning? Did you get any sleep?'

'I'm fine and yes, I slept okay. I'm sorry I scared you, don't worry about me.'

'Of course I'm going to worry, I'm your friend. What are you doing today, would you like to come out to lunch with us?'

Caitlin lunched almost every Saturday with a retired ex-police officer, a large buxom woman with platinum blonde hair and a cut-glass accent who looked and sounded intimidating but who was very sweet, terribly nosy and incredibly intuitive. Melanie would rather have stuck needles in her eyes than go to lunch where her story would have been winkled out in seconds. 'No, thanks,' she said, bringing up a lie she knew her friend would believe. 'I really need to get some work done.'

'Okay, then I'll give you a ring later, check you don't need anything.'

She didn't want to sound ungrateful, but Melanie would have preferred to be left alone. 'Lovely, thanks, you're so good to me.'

'That's what friends are for,' Caitlin said and hung up.

Melanie put the handset down and looked across at her mobile. There was no point in putting it off but that didn't stop her from doing just that, sitting looking balefully across the room as if the mobile were something that had offended her. Finally, she stood and picked it up.

Her bark of laughter was followed by a fit of giggles that bore a trace of hysteria. She clamped a hand over her mouth and took a shuddering breath. There was nothing funny about it. The phone was dead; she'd forgotten to charge it.

Plugging it in, she could have checked the emails then but

couldn't bring herself to look. She left it to charge and went to make some coffee. She'd no intention of doing any work. Truth was, there was nothing she really needed to do. But sitting around worrying and allowing herself to be consumed with fear – that wasn't an option.

She thought about ringing one of her other friends to meet for coffee, dismissing the idea almost immediately. Small talk over coffee wasn't going to be enough of a diversion. But she wasn't going to sit around. She'd go into the city, look at the fashion, maybe buy some new clothes.

Forced optimism kept her going until the reality of Oxford Street hit her. Crowded, as usual, she should have been able to hide in the normality of it all but instead fear lurked around every shop corner and in every person who accidently bumped into her. She'd only walked a short distance from the underground station when she realised what a silly idea it had been and when a passing available taxi caught her eye, she jumped at the chance to escape. With a wave of her hand it pulled over, and seconds later she was slumped in the back seat.

She was almost home when the taxi stopped at the traffic lights at the corner of her road, her gaze drifting automatically down the street to the front of her apartment. Bloom Park Road was normally a quiet residential street; she rarely saw anyone, and never anyone hanging about. But now, her eyes widened as she saw someone lounging on her garden wall. A male figure. Hugo? She pressed her nose to the window, but he was too far away to identify for sure. All she could be certain of was that it was a man.

18

Melanie reached forward to knock loudly on the partition that separated her from the driver. Too loudly, startling a yelp from him. He turned to look at her with an angry expression that faded when he saw her wide eyes. 'What the hell's going on?'

'Drive on. Don't turn! Straight, go straight on.' She waved at the road ahead.

'Okay, okay,' he said, indicating to pull into the other lane, driving straight through when the lights changed with a hand raised in thanks to the car behind. 'Where to?'

She strained against her seatbelt to turn and stare out the rear windscreen as if she expected the man to be running after her.

'Where to?' the driver repeated, his voice louder, irritated.

'Take the next left, then left at the end of that road. I want you to drive slowly past the other end of my road, okay?'

There was silence before he agreed. 'Is there someone there you're worried about? You want me to ring the police?'

'No, no,' she hurried to reassure him. 'It's my... my brother...

he's always coming around to borrow money. If it's him, I don't want him to see me.'

The taxi driver, obviously feeling he'd done his bit, gave a casual shrug, followed her directions and a couple of minutes later they were approaching the other end of Bloom Park Road. Melanie slid down in the seat to stay out of view. 'Can you go as slowly as possible,' she said.

'I'll do my best,' the driver said, 'but I can't for very long, this is a busy road.'

She didn't bother replying, straining to see out the window. Her apartment was closer to this end of the road, she could make out the figure more clearly. Definitely not Hugo, too bulky, maybe a little shorter. Unfortunately, he was looking in the other direction and wore a hat pulled down low so it was impossible to tell who he was. Lack of recognition, however, did nothing to diminish her fear.

'Where now?' The driver sounded bored.

'Drop me here,' she said, sitting up.

When the taxi pulled away, she stood in indecision. If she walked back to look again, she might meet him coming towards her but she couldn't just stand there either. It wasn't Hugo, but she already knew he wasn't her greatest fear. What if it were *nobody*? *Time to pay.* There had been no demands for money, so it could only mean one thing, couldn't it? A life for a life. She shivered; her light jacket and thin blouse weren't meant for standing around on a chilly day. Folding her arms across her chest, for warmth as much as protection, she walked towards her road, anxiety making her footsteps jerky and slow.

She stopped at the corner of a high garden wall that wrapped around onto Bloom Park Road and leaning against it, peered around, confused when, as far as she could see, the road was empty.

Maybe, he'd gone to ring her doorbell. She stepped back, waited a few seconds, and looked again. But there was nobody there. He'd given up and gone away. Hadn't he? She moved forward slowly, her eyes constantly scanning the street ahead. When she was halfway along, she took a deep breath and ran. She pulled her key from her bag as she moved, had it in her hand, desperately prodding the keyhole with it when she got to her front door, missing in her haste, the key screeching as it scratched the metal. She was afraid to look behind and tried again, her fingers clumsy with sweat. This time she succeeded. Turning the key, she pushed the door open, stumbled into the hall and slammed the door behind her.

She couldn't go further and slumped against the wall, trying to catch her breath. There had been someone there, he must have walked in the other direction. She was not imagining things.

It was several minutes before she felt able to move, keeping a hand on the wall as she walked to the lounge.

Her mobile was still plugged into the charger. Because it had been completely flat, she had to key in her password to start it again and, when she did, it pinged manically with all the missed calls and messages. Quite a few of the missed calls were from Caitlin, starting early morning, then a long pause, and more within the last hour. Melanie would ring her back when she had the energy. All the other calls were from a withheld number.

Leaving it, she checked her emails. Nothing more from *nobody*. Nothing from Hugo... no surprise there. Sinking onto the sofa, she looked at the list of missed calls again. Twelve in total. Someone really wanted to get hold of her but they hadn't bothered to leave a message, voicemail, or text and since the number was withheld, there was no way for her to ring back.

Time to pay. The words rattled in her head. Was this the

idea? To have her so unsettled, so damn scared that she did what Cherry had done?

If it was the man in the street, might he come back? Melanie hurried to the bedroom, slanting the shutters to peer out. As far as she could see, the road was empty. She closed the shutters and, for good measure, pulled the heavy curtains she only ever used in the depths of winter. Once that was done, she went into the spare bedroom and did the same.

The back of the house looked out onto a small walled courtyard. There was no entrance, the walls over six foot high. She was safe here. Wasn't she? When her mobile rang, she caught her breath and froze. *It could be him.* It stopped and started again. Then her house phone rang. Her breath coming out in a whoosh, she grabbed it. 'Hello?'

'Where the hell have you been, I've been ringing your mobile?' Caitlin's anxious voice, loud and comforting.

'The battery was flat,' Melanie said, telling a half-truth. 'Sorry, I'm not long in, actually. I'd decided to do some shopping.'

'And how are you feeling?'

Terrified. 'Fine,' she said, hoping her friend wouldn't hear the tremble in her voice. When a sigh brushed her ear, she knew Caitlin guessed she was upset. She just wouldn't know the real reason.

'Would you like me to come over?'

Melanie put some steel in her voice. 'No, honestly, I'm fine, a bit tired, maybe shopping hadn't been the best idea. I'm planning to settle down and watch one of those Netflix series I've been meaning to watch for absolutely ages.'

'If you're sure?'

'Positive, but thank you, Caitlin, you're a good friend.'

'Yes, well I worry about you. Ring me tomorrow night so I know you're doing okay.'

With the promise made, Melanie hung up and sat back. The heating was on, the apartment was warm, and suddenly a waft of body odour hit her. She stank of despair and fear.

A long hot shower left her feeling fresher but no more relaxed. She pulled on a pair of pyjamas and sat on the sofa to watch television, switching it on, then getting up to make herself a cup of tea and something to eat. She hadn't the energy or desire to cook, settling in the end for some cheese and crackers.

The news was blaring as she carried the mug and plate into the lounge. Watching the headlines with little interest, she drank her tea, ignored the crackers and nibbled on some cheese. It took a while to choose which series she wanted to watch, then she changed her mind and switched to a channel showing reruns of *Frasier*. She'd seen them all before, but they were amusing, unthreatening candyfloss for her brain. She even managed a chuckle.

A noise jerked her upright. She reached for the remote, muted the television and cocked her head to listen. When it came again, she tried to identify what it was, where it came from. Holding her breath, she stood. It seemed to be coming from the kitchen. From the open doorway of the lounge, she looked across the hall. The kitchen was in darkness, and for the moment it was silent. Then it came again, a dull metallic sound.

Adrenaline shot through her, causing a spike of anger that dislodged the fear. She stepped across the hall, reached inside for the light switch and blinked as the room filled with light. The metallic sound came again. Her hand went to her neck, then she laughed, a sad laugh at her stupidity, the sound full of hopelessness. She'd thrown the foil that had covered the cheese into the sink and her tap dripped. That's all it was, the metallic sound of a drop of water landing on tinfoil.

With the tinfoil in the bin, quiet was restored. Melanie's

spurt of anger had faded, and fear once again simmered. There was a magnetic strip on the kitchen wall holding a set of expensive knives she'd bought herself as a house-warming present, intent then on taking up cordon bleu cookery as a hobby. She hadn't and most of the knives had never been used. The middle one was the biggest with a sharp twenty-centimetre blade. She pulled it from the magnetic strip and took it with her when she went back to the lounge, feeling safer with it sitting beside her, and later she fell asleep with it lying beside her pillow.

To her surprise, she managed to get several hours sleep. She followed her usual Sunday routine and went out to the local shop for a newspaper, bringing it home and reading it over breakfast. She'd been invited to a friend's house for lunch, a casual invitation to an open-house affair. She decided against going, sending her friend a text message explaining she was too busy with work. Her friend, in the same line of business, would understand completely.

Instead, staying indoors, safe, Melanie settled with the box set of *Downton Abbey*, a series she'd never watched but that had been recommended to her. It was the perfect choice but even as she enjoyed it, her eyes constantly flitted to where her phone sat. It stayed quiet, but there was no peace in the silence.

That night, once again, she slept with the knife beside her pillow. She woke several times and listened for a sound in the quiet, her hand creeping around the cold handle as if it were a talisman to ward off the evil. She would be comforted for a moment and slip back to sleep, only to fall into that same awful dream she'd had for years and jolt awake again.

~

In the morning, slightly heavier makeup disguised her pallor and concealer hid the dark shadows under her eyes. With her hair neatly pinned up in her customary chignon and wearing a dark-grey suit, she looked almost normal. She didn't think anyone would notice that her eyes never seemed to sit still, and the way the simplest sound set her on edge. There were no meetings planned for that day, she could stay in her safe, secure office away from prying eyes.

Normally, she took the tube to work but the thought that *nobody* might be among the people surrounding her made her shiver. Instead, she called a taxi, waiting until it was pulled up outside before taking the safety chain off the front door. She didn't step out until she'd glanced up and down the road, then made a run for the car door and jumped inside.

When she pushed through the front door of her office building, the first thing that struck her was how normal everything was. The usual greetings from the front-of-house staff, the friendly wave from Dan the security man, the *Did you have a nice weekend* from several people she passed. Everyone was going about their day as if everything was hunky-dory. Or maybe, like her, they were all pretending.

She shut her office door and pressed her forehead against it for a moment. It was going to be a long day. Behind her desk, she was tempted to cross her arms on the cool wood, rest her head in the crook of her elbow and shut her eyes. Instead, she switched on her computer and tried to concentrate her mind on work.

There was an email from Richard, sent, she was surprised to see, at five that morning. She opened it, the tension easing as she read. He'd spoken to the CEO's of both Fanton's and City-East and explained the situation to them following which, the email informed her, an agreement to delay the merger had been made. She doubted if either had been happy and wondered what promises Richard had had to make to ensure their compliance.

It took her a few minutes to compose a suitably grateful reply. There were a few more emails to deal with and a couple of reports to read, gritty eyes struggling to stay focused.

Late morning, she headed to the staffroom for coffee, drinking a mugful and refilling it. Caffeine might be the only way to get through the day. With the mug in her hand, she opened the door to head back to her office.

'Hello.'

Melanie's hand jerked and the overfilled mug tilted, spilling coffee down the side. She swore softly as the hot coffee hit her hand.

'Here, let me,' Liam Quinn said, pulling tissues from his pocket. He handed her one and bent to mop the drops of coffee from the floor. 'I'm sorry. I didn't mean to startle you.'

Melanie used the tissue he'd given her to wipe her hand and the side of the mug. 'I wasn't expecting anyone to be lurking outside the door.'

'I wasn't lurking,' he said evenly. He nodded towards the end of the corridor. 'I was heading for the lift.'

She shifted the mug in her hand and held the damp tissue in the other. It wasn't fair to blame him because she'd been distracted. It wasn't his fault that the slightest thing made her jump. 'Yes, I'm sorry, it was my fault. Thanks for coming to my rescue.'

With a nod, she left him standing there and returned to her office. Too restless to sit, she stood at the window and sipped her coffee. The day was already fading but the street below was bright with the lights from the ground floor offices. There was the usual hustle and bustle around the front door, her eyes drifting unfocused over the moving bodies before seeing one slouched against the wall that made her gasp. Recognition was instantaneous – the same heavy coat and hat pulled down low over his eyes. It was the man from outside her apartment.

Her reaction was instinctive. She put her coffee down, pulled her office door open and stepped out. 'Mr Quinn,' she called to the man who was jabbing the lift button impatiently. 'Could I have a word, please?'

'I have another job for you,' she said, when he approached, her voice trembling slightly. Inside her office, she walked to the window and pointed. 'See that man leaning against the wall? The one with the hat pulled down over his head?'

Quinn took a step closer. 'I see him,' he said, turning to look at her, a frown between his eyes.

'I want to know who he is.' She moved away from the window and folded her arms across her chest. 'He's following me. He was outside my house yesterday. I don't know what he wants, can you find out?'

Quinn stared at her without speaking, his eyes assessing. 'I can try. You want me to come back and tell you?'

Did she? If he were seen coming in and out of her office, would that give rise to the kind of gossip she'd tried for so many years to avoid? 'No,' she said. 'I have your card, I'll ring you later.'

Without another word, Quinn was gone.

She moved back to the window and watched as Quinn exited the front door a few minutes later. He looked up and down the street before he approached the slouching man. From where Melanie stood, it was impossible to see either man's expression. Initially, the man stayed slumped against the wall and showed no reaction to whatever Quinn was saying but then, to her surprise, he threw his head back... in laughter? The light from the office windows cast strange shadows, it was impossible to make out what was happening. But after a few minutes the man pushed away from the wall and he and Quinn walked off together and were soon outside her line of vision.

19

For only the second time since she'd started to work for Masters, Melanie left work at five on the dot. It was stupid to feel guilty; there was nothing else for her to do.

Her coat hung on the back of the door. She took it down and slipped it on, belting it tightly, her mind on Quinn. The faith in her ability to make correct judgements about people had taken a battering thanks to Hugo, but Quinn struck her as one of the good ones. Or maybe she hoped he was. She sighed, grabbed her briefcase, switched off the light and headed out.

Although she'd watched the slouching man heading away in Quinn's company, she still hesitated in reception. She was reluctant to leave in case the unknown man had returned and was waiting for her. Dan, one of the security guards, was standing by the exit. He was always pleasant and friendly, she didn't mind asking him a favour. 'I'm trying to avoid an ex,' she said quietly, 'and I'm sure I saw him hanging around earlier, would you check outside for me?'

Dan drew his shoulders back. 'Of course, wait here.'

Melanie moved to the window as he stepped outside. Instead of giving a casual check, she watched him walk to the end of the building and look around, then back to the other end to do the same. She smiled and took a deep breath. Another one of the good ones – she had to keep reminding herself they existed.

'Coast is clear, Ms Scott,' he said, coming back inside, a dusting of raindrops on his shoulders and cap.

'It's Melanie,' she said, for the umpteenth time. 'Thanks, I appreciate that.'

He looked at her sternly. 'You should go to the police if a man is stalking you, Ms Scott. You need to keep safe.'

She rested a hand briefly on his arm. 'Thank you, Dan. It's not an issue, honestly. I didn't want to have to speak to him today.' It wasn't the man outside you had to protect yourself from, she could have told him, it was the one you invited in. The one she'd trusted. She conjured up a warm smile for Dan and left before it faded.

Outside, she swore softly. She should have ordered a taxi. The chances of an available one passing at this time of the day were slim, but she stood a moment in hope before shaking her head and heading towards the underground. As usual, it was noisy and crowded. She was eager to hear what Quinn had discovered about the man but standing in a packed commuter train wasn't the time or place for what might be a nerve-wracking conversation. With her briefcase wedged between her feet, she quickly sent a simple text. *Did you find out who he was?*

It wasn't until she was walking the short distance between the station and her home, eyes darting right and left, feet clicking speedily along the pathway that her phone beeped. It was from Quinn, an irritatingly short and uninformative text. *Yes, best we meet.* She groaned in frustration. Why was nothing ever simple anymore.

She tried to think of a suitable place to meet. Only a few days ago, she'd have thought nothing of asking him to her home. Not now though, no matter that she thought he was one of the good guys, it would be a while before she'd leave herself that vulnerable again. She didn't know many places suitable to meet, in fact, she knew only one.

She waited until she was inside her apartment before she replied. *The Fulham Arms, on the corner of Fulham and Cassidy Road in an hour.*

There was no reply; she took it as agreement.

The pub was only a ten-minute walk from her apartment. She changed from her work suit into casual jeans, a jumper and comfortable walking shoes – ones she could run in if necessary. Who she'd be running from she'd no idea but it seemed better to be prepared.

It was too early to leave; she didn't want to sit alone in the pub so she made coffee, sliced chunks of cheese and sat watching the news, one eye on the kitchen clock. Quinn struck her as the kind of person who would arrive on time. She left the apartment five minutes before the appointed hour, then walked briskly, eyes constantly scanning.

The Fulham Arms was an old pub whose only attempt at modernisation was the introduction of a limited menu of pie and chips or beer-battered haddock and chips. But the banquettes and chairs were comfortable, the place was clean and the lighting soft and subtle. She'd only been inside once, several years before, on a first date with a guy she'd met at a conference. She couldn't remember his name, or why she'd never seen him again.

Inside, the place hadn't changed. The lighting was as she'd remembered, perhaps a little dimmer. With her eyes adjusting to the light, she looked around for Quinn. The pub was quiet, background music, murmurs of conversation, the occasional guffaw from a man in the corner trying too hard to impress the woman beside him. Melanie's eyes flickered over them all nervously before seeing the man she was looking for. He'd taken a table opposite the door in a corner lit by a lamp to one side. Its shade was smoked glass and gave little light. It hid his expression and, wary, she hesitated before approaching.

He'd been early, the pint glass on the table before him almost empty 'Can I get you another?' she asked as she reached him, in lieu of apologising for being late.

She turned away without a word when he nodded. At the bar, she ordered a mineral water for herself. 'And whatever it is he's drinking,' she said, pointing to where Quinn sat.

As the barman pulled the pint, she could feel Quinn's eyes on her, checking her out. It was an uncomfortable sensation, but two could play at that game and she gave him the once-over as she made her way back to the table. He'd taken off his jacket, loosened his tie and looked like a man comfortable in his skin, a self-confidence she'd noticed the first time they'd met. 'Here you go,' she said, putting the pint on the table before taking the seat opposite.

'That looks very much like water you're drinking,' Quinn said as his fingers circled the pint.

'Good detective work.' She didn't need to explain her choice of drink. This wasn't a date, a getting to know you first meeting. This was business. 'So,' she said, 'as you've noticed, I'm not into pleasantries, what have you to tell me about the man?'

Before he answered, he lifted his glass and took two long swallows, half-emptying it. He wiped his mouth with a hand and looked across the table. 'It was the man whose work address we found for you. Eric Thomas. Edgware Motors.'

She had her fingers around her glass of water, they tightened automatically when she heard the name. That was who it was! She hadn't recognised him, fooled by a heavy coat and a stupid hat.

'What he said didn't mean much to me but maybe, since you know him, it does to you.' Quinn looked at her intently. 'He said... and I'm quoting verbatim here... "I wanted to reassure her that I'd no intention of causing her any harm, that I never had".'

That was it? That's why she'd been going crazy? She picked up her glass and took a mouthful of water. Perhaps if she hadn't had Hugo so firmly in her head, she would have recognised Eric when he'd stood outside her house. She swirled the water around the glass, a frown creasing her brow as she thought about what Quinn had said. Wasn't there something a bit odd about this? She hadn't needed the reassurance; she'd believed him when he said he hadn't been involved. Now, it was almost a case of protesting his innocence too much.

'He was surprised he'd worried you,' Quinn went on. 'You gave me the impression he'd been stalking you but he insisted he'd only called to your house once and this was his first day to call to your office.' He leaned forward. 'Did you think it was someone else?'

She sighed. 'Initially, I did, I thought it was... someone I didn't want to see again. It never crossed my mind it would be Eric, perhaps it should have done.' The missed calls, she'd given him her phone number, it must have been him trying to contact her. She played with her glass, rolling it between her hands.

'When I told him I'd pass his message on, he said you wouldn't hear from him again.' Quinn crossed his arms. 'I don't suppose you're going to tell me what it's about, are you?'

She shook her head. 'It was nothing, a mix-up over something that happened a long time ago.'

Quinn didn't look convinced but instead of pressing her he switched the conversation. 'This other guy? He's been bothering you?'

She met his eyes; they were kind, sympathetic even. A brace for her backbone, isn't that how she'd viewed his strength the first time they'd met? 'The police are dealing with it.'

'The police?' His voice was surprised, eyes narrowing. 'So more serious than just bothering you?'

How did they end up talking about Hugo? 'He stole something from me,' she said. It was the easiest way to explain.

Quinn seemed to process this, his eyes growing hard. 'He broke in?' Her silence appeared to be enough of an answer. 'You let him in?'

'I let him in,' she agreed. 'Foolish perhaps, but not a crime.' She had to keep reminding herself of that. Stupidity wasn't a crime. Hoping and believing in happy ever after wasn't a crime.

She stared down at her glass, tilting it backwards and forwards to make the water swirl. It was a few seconds before she looked up and caught his eyes. They were looking at her with such sympathy and sadness that despite her reservations, she found herself telling him about Hugo. 'I was ghosted,' she said, finishing her story. 'A whole new experience for me.'

'I suppose, in the way these things usually go, he's hidden his tracks well?'

'Fake email address, fake website, probably a fake name too for all I know.'

'These days, every bugger knows how to set up fake accounts.' Draining his pint, Quinn nodded towards her glass. 'Would you like something stronger?'

'A whisky,' she said, deciding she needed it. 'A Lagavulin if they have it?'

If he seemed surprised by her choice, by her exacting request, he didn't show it and returned a few minutes later with another pint and a small glass that he set down in front of her. 'I'm glad you're paying me well,' he said, 'you've got expensive taste.'

Picking it up, she sniffed the amber liquid. 'I don't drink much but I was in a pub recently and asked the barman to recommend something. This is what he suggested.' She took a minute sip; it was as good as she remembered. She felt his eyes on her and looked up. 'What?'

'There's a lot of new terminology bandied about to cover social media experiences, both negative and positive. You mentioned you'd been ghosted–'

'Isn't that what it's called?' she interrupted. 'Years ago, I'd simply have said I was dumped. But the way he appeared to vanish sounded like what I'd read about ghosting, and my friend Caitlin agreed.' Melanie took another sip of whisky. 'I'd read about it, but never thought I'd be a victim.'

'I'm not sure you and your friend were right,' Quinn said, picking up his pint.

'She's a detective inspector with the Metropolitan Police service. She knows what she's talking about.'

His eyes narrowed. 'I'm sure she does but perhaps she didn't know about the theft of the information at that stage. It sounds to me more like a case of *catfishing*.'

'What the hell is catfishing?' Melanie had seen catfish once, on a holiday in India, twenty or thirty of them in a pool waiting to be fed, an open-mouthed frenzy that had given her the heebie-jeebies. Surely there wasn't a connection?

'It's another social media problem,' Quinn explained. 'A predator fabricates a false identity in order to deceive or defraud. They normally target specific individuals – the lonely, wealthy woman, for instance. Or'– he waved a hand towards her – 'someone who may be in possession of potentially lucrative information.'

Melanie picked up her glass and knocked back the remainder of the whisky. Hadn't she thought from the start that Hugo had been too good to be true? Now she knew why. He'd targeted her from the very beginning. Sadly, it all made perfect sense now.

'Were you able to give the police a good description?' Quinn asked, interrupting her thoughts.

'I didn't need to.' She reached for her phone, brought up Hugo's photo and handed it to him. 'It's the one that was on his website, I'd taken a screenshot to show my friend so I was able to send it to them.' She saw Quinn's suddenly alert expression and frowned. 'Do you recognise him?'

'No,' he said, but the frown didn't fade. He handed her back the phone, picked up his pint and drank deeply. 'Don't be too disappointed if the police aren't able to locate him. They're usually limited by manpower and resources. Anyway, if the merger is delayed, this Hugo person will probably offload the shares for something more instantly lucrative. These guys are rarely in it for the long haul.'

Melanie nodded. It was the outcome they were hoping for. Suddenly curious she asked, 'Could you find him?'

Quinn considered her request for a moment before tilting his head side to side. 'I'd love to be able to say yes, to claim James-Bond-style powers, but the reality is, probably not. From what you've told me, this guy is intelligent. He'll have covered his tracks well.' He gave a slight shrug. 'I could give it a try.'

Find him, tear his eyes out, make him suffer. She sighed, felt his eyes on her again, warm with understanding. 'No, it's not necessary. He's finished with me now and moved on, I'd be better off to forget about him.'

'That's one of the reasons these people get away with it,' Quinn said, sounding as if he were disappointed with her reply. 'Con men like Hugo wreak havoc with people's lives without ever being brought to justice. You should take a stand.'

'No,' she said firmly, 'it's best to leave it to the police.' She reached for her jacket and pulled it on. 'If they can't, well so be it. Now, I must go. Thank you for that information and for dealing with Eric. And as before, I'd appreciate if the invoice for your time is sent to me personally and not to the Masters account.'

He shrugged. 'No problem. At least now, you know he's nothing to worry about.'

She had to bite her tongue on the words she wanted to say. Wanted to beg him to walk home with her, maybe even to stay so that she could wrap his confidence around her, steal it to keep her safe. Instead, she turned and walked through the now-busy pub to the door. Outside, it was colder and heavy rain bounced off the pavement. Passing cars sent up a spray of dirty water, windscreen wipers going shush, shush, shush as drivers battled to see in the deluge.

It was only a ten-minute walk back to her apartment. The lurking man had been Eric trying to reassure her. Everything was okay. According to Quinn, she'd nothing to be afraid of.

But, of course, he didn't know everything. *Time to pay*. She had every reason to be very, very afraid.

20

It was only a ten-minute walk, but the heavy rain ran down Melanie's showerproof jacket and soaked into her jeans. She walked quickly, ignoring the puddles underfoot and the discomfort of cold rainwater soaking her feet. Her eyes were never still. On a night like tonight everyone looked suspicious. People were mummified with hats and scarfs, they peered from behind umbrellas, and aggressively hogged the inside of the pavement to avoid being splashed by the passing traffic. Wet surfaces shimmered in both street lights and car headlights, causing the shadows that lay across the path and roads to flicker and dance.

It was all scarily unsettling. Finally reaching her front door, she gave a last anxious glance around before pushing it open and hurrying to shut and lock it behind her. Twenty minutes later, wrapped in her robe, she remembered her promise to ring Caitlin and picked up her phone. She was unable to resist checking her emails, relieved to see there was nothing new.

'Hi,' she said when it was answered.

'Hi yourself,' Caitlin said. 'I was about to ring. You got through the day okay?'

'Yes, it was fine. Nothing's going to happen with the merger now for a while so it's relatively quiet.' The conversation slipped into general chit-chat but Melanie's mind was on the meeting she'd had with Quinn. Could she really trust him? She waited until Caitlin finished a long involved story about one of her colleagues and the affair he was having with a married junior minister. 'It'll come out, these things always do,' Melanie said. She looked at her phone in annoyance when it beeped. 'My battery is going flat, can you ring me on the house phone?' She hung up when Caitlin agreed and picked up the handset when it rang.

'You need a new mobile,' Caitlin said and proceeded to launch into a description of the latest on the market.

Melanie contributed a hmmm and uh-huh now and then, waiting for the opportunity to slip her request into the conversation. Finally, into a lull, and as smoothly as she could, she dropped, 'By the way, you know that private investigation service we use, Rabbie and Henderson?'

'Sure, they're one of the best around.'

'They've taken on a new investigator, I met him in the staffroom earlier.' The lie came easily. 'Seems like a nice guy, an ex-copper, I wondered if you'd heard of him. Liam Quinn. Tall, broad-shouldered guy with grey eyes.'

'Oh, you noticed his eyes, did you? Nice-looking, is he?'

'Don't be stupid,' Melanie said, more sharply than she'd intended, immediately regretting being rude. She pressed a hand over her forehead. 'I'm sorry, Caitlin. He's new. I want to make sure we can trust him. I suppose I'll be second-guessing myself for a while thanks to Hugo.'

'That's completely understandable,' Caitlin said. 'I don't know a Liam Quinn, but I'll ask around if it will make things easier for you.'

'You're a good friend.'

'So you keep saying, and as your friend, I'm suggesting you should go see a counsellor. That bastard did a number on you.'

Melanie remembered what the last counsellor she'd visited had said and repeated it to her friend. 'They don't offer a magic get-out-of-jail-free card, you know, Caitlin. Anyway, honestly, I'm fine. It's not the first time I've been let down by a guy, after all.'

'Okay.' The word was dragged out, full of doubt. 'If you need me, Mel, you know I'm here for you.'

'Thank you, I know, and I really do appreciate it.'

They chatted a while longer about nothing in particular before they began their goodbyes.

'You promise to ring if you need me,' Caitlin said.

'I promise, I promise, now goodbye, and thank you again.'

Melanie hung up. It was early but she was so tired bed seemed the best place to be. She snuggled under the duvet, her hand creeping under the pillow to hold the knife that still lay there, her talisman, its solid handle giving her comfort.

She wasn't sure how long she'd been asleep when she heard the doorbell, and opened her eyes, startled. Had she imagined it? Then it came again, longer this time, a double ring, someone very impatient or very determined to wake her. The message from *nobody* flashed in her head, an internal neon light. *Time to pay*. Was this it?

No, that didn't make sense. He was hardly going to ring the doorbell. But somebody was. She swung her feet to the floor, grabbed her robe from the back of the door and pulled it on. Brushing tangled hair back with trembling hands, she stepped out into the hallway. The front door was solid, no indication of who stood on the other side. She moved closer and yelped with fright when the doorbell sounded again, stumbling the last couple of steps to lean against the door and press her ear to it.

They must have been listening and heard her yelp. 'Ms Scott? Are you there? It's the police, Ms Scott, DI Elliot.'

Recognising his voice, on a whoosh of relief, she fumbled with the safety chain, undid the lock and opened the door. 'Sorry,' she said, standing back to let him and a short, stocky woman into the hall. 'I was asleep, you startled me.'

Elliot tilted his head towards the woman at his side. 'This is DS Burke.'

Melanie smiled at her. It wasn't returned and her own faded in response. Only then did she begin to wonder why the police were calling on her at... 'What time *is* it?'

'A little after three,' Elliot said. 'Would you mind if we sat down?'

Three in the morning? Melanie looked at him in confusion before waving them both through to the kitchen. She felt as though she'd wandered into one of those crime series that she watched too often. It seemed to be her turn to speak. 'Would you like some tea? Or coffee?'

'No, thanks,' Elliot answered for them both.

Deciding she needed something, resisting the temptation to shock them by going next door and bringing back the whisky, Melanie filled the kettle and clicked the switch. She could feel their eyes on her, she'd no idea what was going on but she knew the police calling at this crazy hour could only be something bad.

Sitting with a strong mug of coffee, she looked at Sam Elliot. He'd been friendly, kind even, when he'd called on Friday. Today, his expression was guarded. 'Should I be calling my solicitor?' Another line from a television series, it seemed appropriate.

'Why, do you think you need one?' DS Burke said. The detective had bad teeth, her eyes were sharp and mean and she was looking at Melanie as if she knew she was guilty of something.

'I don't, it seemed to be the thing to say.' She ran a hand

through her hair. This wasn't television and it was three in the morning. 'What do you want?'

'Where were you this evening?' DI Elliot asked. He wasn't looking as sympathetically at Melanie as the last time they'd met, but he was wearing that terrible tie again. It showed he had a heart.

'I was out with a friend for a drink.' It was only a little white lie to call Quinn a friend, saying she'd been out with a private investigator might lead to questions she didn't want to answer.

'What time did you get home?'

She frowned, trying to remember. 'I'm not exactly sure, around nine.'

'And you've been here since?'

'Yes.' She watched them exchange glances but they gave nothing away.

'Did you bring your *friend* back with you?' There was a sneer on the word 'friend' and a suggestion in the small eyes. DS Burke was one of those people who made everything sound sordid.

Melanie didn't answer, looking back to Elliot instead. 'I'd like to know what this is about, please?'

Suddenly, DS Burke gave a satisfied smirk. She lifted her hand and pointed towards the kitchen. 'There's a knife missing,' she said, indicating the row of knives with the glaring gap in the middle. 'Can you tell us where it is?'

Of course, Melanie could, she knew exactly where it was, but what did it say about her that she slept with a knife beside her pillow? Seeing the hard look in Burke's eyes, Melanie knew she wasn't going to let it go. 'It's in the bedroom, I can go and get it if you really want to see it?'

'Maybe you could show us?'

Reluctantly, she led the way. It was a cosy, pretty room with rosebud-sprigged wallpaper, white linen on the bed and the slightly muggy smell of night-time bedrooms anywhere. All looked perfectly normal except for the knife. Its dull black handle and long, gleaming blade was dark and lethal and totally out of place beside her pillow.

'Well, how about that,' DS Burke said, a gleam in her eye as she fished disposable gloves from her pocket and reached to pick it up. She peered along its length, unable to prevent disappointment crossing her features. 'It looks clean,' she admitted, looking at Elliot.

Melanie was going to assure her it *was* clean, that it had never been used but stopped herself in time. Was this what it was all about? Was she under suspicion for having stabbed someone? *Time to pay.* Was she going to be framed for a murder she hadn't committed?

'Why do you keep it here?' Elliot asked.

'I was feeling a bit nervous,' she said, trying to keep her voice firm, and because she'd really had enough, she added, 'It's not against the law, is it?' Leaving that floating in the air, she headed back to the kitchen and sat in the same chair. She heard Burke give an unattractive snort, then the low murmur of voices before both officers rejoined her. Burke laid the knife carefully on the kitchen counter before taking her seat.

DI Elliot's eyes were grave as he looked at her. 'Getting back to the question DS Burke asked a while ago, did your friend come home with you?'

Melanie shook her head, pressing her lips together to stop them trembling.

'Okay,' Elliot said slowly. 'Did you, by any chance, speak to anyone after you got home?'

Relief almost made her smile. 'Actually, I did. I rang my friend, Caitlin.' She looked at DS Burke who was writing in a dog-eared notebook. 'That's Detective Inspector Caitlin Ballantyne, by the way.' She took a great deal of pleasure in seeing the writing stop abruptly.

'What time was that at?' Elliot said, his expression less grim.

'Around ten. It'll be on my mobile, I can get it and show you.'

'That would be helpful,' he said with a slight smile.

She didn't move. 'I think I've been very co-operative and I *will* get my phone to show you but not until you tell me what's going on.'

Elliot leaned closer, his elbows resting on his knees. 'We've identified Hugo Field,' he said softly. 'His real name is Oscar Franklin. He has been arrested a number of times for fraud but he's a slippery customer and has always managed to avoid prison.'

Melanie released her breath in a long sigh. 'This time he won't, will he?'

Elliot shook his head. 'I'm afraid he won't be going to prison this time either, he's been murdered. His body was found in Richmond Park at midnight. He'd been stabbed.'

21

In a daze, Melanie found her phone and handed it to DI Elliot who made a note of the time of her call. 'We were given an unofficial time of death,' he told her, handing it back, 'approximately eleven pm. Just after you were speaking to your friend. It looks like you have a good alibi.'

'Not that I want to be a suspect,' she said, frowning, 'but how can you be so sure. Maybe, I took my phone with me.'

He shook his head. 'Mobile coverage in Richmond Park is notoriously unreliable and patchy. I will, of course, be having a word with Inspector Ballantyne but I'd imagine she'll confirm that your call was uninterrupted, won't she?'

'Of course, she will. Actually, my phone was going flat and I asked her to ring me on my home number so that's even more certain.' Melanie was horrified at the thought that anyone would think she was capable of such violence. Without a doubt, she had wanted to make Hugo pay for deceiving her and had imagined causing him pain and suffering but she was only capable of the thought, not the deed. 'I can't believe I was even considered a suspect.'

'We deal with facts, not emotions, Ms Scott. He deceived you, caused you trouble in your job. It gives you a motive for killing him.'

'He is... was... a big man, I'm not sure I'd have gone after him with a knife.'

'It's perfect weather for it,' DS Burke said, looking at the knife. 'Hide that under your coat, get close enough, whip it out and stick it in. A woman could easily have done it.'

Melanie looked at her aghast. Surely it wasn't that easy to kill someone? Then she dropped her head, shutting her eyes on the memory that had never gone away, never faded with the years, that young Robert Redford lookalike, Matthew Thomas. She above all people should know that it was unbelievably easy to kill if you used the appropriate weapon. A sharp blade or lethal, ruinous rumours. Both equally dangerous and fatal. There was a heavy weight of guilt in her chest. Her throat thickened and she prayed the detectives would leave before she fell apart. She could feel their eyes on her and didn't want to look up to see Elliot's sympathy or Burke's derision.

'That's all for the moment,' Elliot said. 'You have my card, if there's anything that comes to you, please ring me.'

She lifted her head, and met his eyes with a slight smile, then watched as Burke, with exaggerated care, put the knife into an oversized evidence bag. It seemed an unnecessary thing to do; hadn't Melanie an alibi? She couldn't summon up the energy to argue.

'It'll be returned as soon as it's been processed,' Burke said and followed up with the trite, 'It's always best to err on the side of caution.'

Elliot looked as if he wanted to say something. Instead, he shrugged and turned to Melanie with a final, 'We'll be in touch if we have any further questions.' With DS Burke trailing after him, the knife in her hand, he headed out to where his car was parked on the far side of the street.

Melanie didn't wait for him to pull away, she shut the door, locked it, and put the safety chain in place. Switching out the lights, she climbed back into bed feeling as if her world had twisted out of shape. The handsome, debonair man leaning against the bar in Blacks appeared before her eyes in full colour. She could almost hear his voice and felt a pang of sadness that her regret was for the memory, not the man. Who'd have thought that such a good package could contain something so nasty. She wasn't glad he was dead, but she wasn't sorry either.

She managed to fall into a restless sleep, waking before her alarm went off at seven. Caitlin, she knew, would already be up. Reaching for her phone, she pressed the speed dial key for her and waited.

'Mel, you okay?' The voice was a little breathless.

'You've been working out?'

'This body doesn't stay this fabulous without hard work, let me tell you, but I doubt very much if you're ringing me at cock-crow to discuss my fitness regime.'

'No, I had a visit from the police earlier. At three, to be exact.' Caitlin's deafening screeched *what!* in reply, forced her to hold the phone away from her ear. 'Relax, it's okay,' she said and with as little emotion as she could, told her exactly what had happened.

'Bloody hell,' Caitlin said. 'Well, that bastard is no loss to the world.' She gave a quick laugh. 'So, I'm your alibi?'

'Yes, as long as the official time of death doesn't change. And,' she added, remembering the knife that DS Burke had insisted on taking, 'as long as they don't find any blood on the knife.'

There was a pregnant pause. 'They're not going to, are they?'

'No, I scrubbed it really hard,' Melanie said with heavy sarcasm. 'What a thing to ask?'

'Why mention blood in the first place! Honestly, Mel, be

careful what you say, police take things literally in these situations.

'I didn't think I was speaking to the police, I thought I was speaking to my friend, Caitlin.' Melanie felt tears well. She couldn't handle this. 'I have to go,' she said and disconnected. It rang again almost immediately. It was tempting to ignore it but knowing her friend would be feeling guilty, she answered.

'I'm sorry,' Caitlin said instantly. 'Listen, how about we meet after work. I'll call to your office; we can go and get something to eat?'

'I don't know–'

'You have to eat.'

The same words Hugo had used. If she'd stuck to her guns then, maybe things would have turned out differently. Hindsight, the bane of her life.

Agreeing to go for something to eat with Caitlin at five, she hung up and got ready for the day. It was going to be long and tiring.

Luckily, she'd no appointments arranged and there were no meetings to attend. She avoided the staffroom where colleagues might question her pallor and the dark rings under her eyes that makeup didn't hide. Instead, she stayed in her office with the door shut. Although the merger was on hold there were a few lingering issues with other clients that needed to be sorted, resulting in long phone conversations, followed up by extensive and expansive emails. There was enough work to keep her busy and her mind from lingering on Hugo's murder, or dwelling on what *nobody* had meant by, *Time to pay*. Now and then, her eyes would lose focus and she would wonder if Cherry had gone through this and had decided that it was impossible to go on.

Melanie had sworn she wasn't going to go down that road, that she was stronger than Cherry. She almost smiled at her hubris. Now she wasn't so sure.

~

Late afternoon, she yawned and stretched. She was glad she'd let Caitlin persuade her to go out for dinner. When her phone rang, she looked at it, wondering if she should ignore it, then shook her head and picked it up. 'Melanie Scott.'

It was Rona. 'There's a man to see you. A Sam Elliot. He's insisting you'll want to see him.'

'That's fine, send him in. It was something I'd arranged and forgot to add to my diary,' Melanie said, not really caring if the lie was swallowed or not.

The knock on her door, a few seconds later, was so soft that if she hadn't been listening out for it, she wouldn't have heard it. 'Come in,' she called.

DI Elliot came around the edge of the door hesitantly, his eyes raking the room, his expression relaxing when he realised she was alone. 'I was hoping to get you on your own but wasn't sure if you shared an office or what, and I was afraid to ask that rather stern-looking woman.'

'Partners all have their own offices,' she said, waving him to a chair. 'Senior partners have very grand ones, but I guess you're not here to learn about the layout of Masters' offices.'

He shook his head. 'Not that it's not very interesting,' he said with an attempt at humour.

She gave it a quick smile. He was wearing a different but equally ghastly tie. 'Another gift from your daughter,' she asked, waving a finger up and down.

He looked down, then back at her with a grin. 'No,' he said, 'this one is courtesy of my wife. She thinks she's got good taste; I haven't had the heart to tell her otherwise.' He shuffled in his seat. 'But I'm not here to talk about my sartorial splendour either.'

'No, I guessed you weren't.' She felt strangely calm. Maybe it was because of what she'd been thinking of such a short time before, that there was always a way out should she choose to take it. Sometimes, having options, no matter how bad they were made things a little easier.

'I'm investigating a murder, Ms Scott, and I don't have time for treading carefully around people's feelings. So, here's what I'm thinking. It seemed to me that you were devastated by Hugo's betrayal. Given the time frame, it looks as if you are in the clear but there's always the possibility that someone took revenge on your behalf.'

Melanie looked at him in wide-eyed disbelief. 'Seriously? You think I asked someone to kill Hugo for me?'

'You were distraught about the way he used you and about the repercussions for your career.'

She had been upset about Hugo – distraught about Cherry and those terrifying emails. 'I have other things going on in my life,' she said tiredly. 'Yes, I was upset, but no, I didn't ask someone to kill Hugo to get revenge.'

Elliot waited a beat. 'Maybe you didn't need to ask.' He looked at her. 'Who did you tell?'

'Apart from Richard Masters and you, the only person I told was Caitlin.' Melanie raised an eyebrow at him. 'Now, if you want to go and accuse Detective Inspector Ballantyne of murder, you go right ahead.'

'Accuse, no,' he said firmly, 'but I will speak to her, it is–'

'Yes, yes,' she interrupted him testily, 'I know, it's your job. She looked at the clock pointedly. 'Please don't let me delay you any further in the execution of your duties.'

It wasn't until he'd left that Melanie realised, she had lied to the police... not deliberately, and not precisely lied... but there was one other person who she'd told about that night.

Liam Quinn.

She remembered the sadness and sympathy that had

appeared in his eyes when she'd told him about what had happened. And hadn't there been a glimmer of recognition when she'd shown him Hugo's photograph? And what was it he'd said? Something about con men who wreak havoc without ever being brought to justice. His expression had been grim and his voice hard.

He was an ex-copper turned private investigator. Had he also turned vigilante?

Had he recognised Hugo and decided to make him pay?

22

Melanie was still sitting, thinking, when the door opened and Caitlin appeared, her eyes sweeping the small room. 'So, this is it?' she said, pushing the door open wide. 'It's not the biggest, is it?'

'But it's mine and' – Melanie indicated the window behind – 'I can look outside and see what the weather's like.' She'd been in Caitlin's office a couple of times; it was twice the size of hers but windowless and with a low ceiling she had found claustrophobic.

Caitlin walked to the window and peered out. 'You win,' she said, turning. 'You ready to go?'

It wasn't five but suddenly Melanie didn't care. Over the years, she'd probably clocked up thousands of hours of overtime. 'Yes,' she said, shutting her laptop and getting to her feet. She pulled on her coat and smoothed a hand over her hair, stopping with a hand on her head as a memory overwhelmed her... that night in Blacks when she'd been tempted to unpin her hair to attract the handsome man at the bar.

'Don't look so sad,' Caitlin said softly.

Sad? Melanie wasn't sure how she felt anymore; her

emotions had been through the wringer and now the only emotion she was sure of, the one constant, was the fear that simmered beneath the surface. 'My life's a bit of a roller-coaster these days, Caitlin. DI Elliot was in this afternoon, not very long ago actually. He will need to speak to you.'

Caitlin's eyebrows rose. 'He already asked me about the phone call. I confirmed the time and that the reception had been perfect. What more does he want?'

'You said he was a good copper; it seems you were right. He's not willing to ignore what I suppose he'd call his gut instinct.'

'Maybe I'm being unusually slow,' Caitlin said, crossing her arms over her chest, 'but I don't understand.'

Melanie shoved her hands in her pockets. 'I have an alibi but he hasn't given up on his idea that revenge may be the motive for Hugo's murder.' She gave a quick smile. 'He's looking into the possibility that someone killed him in retribution for how he duped me. I told him that the only people who knew about what happened were you and Richard.'

'More likely to have been me than Richard,' Caitlin said, and held her hand up quickly. 'And no, in case you have any doubts, I love you dearly but I wouldn't kill for you.'

Melanie laughed and gave her a nudge. 'Good to know! Let's get out of here.'

By unspoken consent, they walked to a small Italian restaurant ten minutes from the office, a place they'd been to before where they were assured of a quiet table and good food. The Sicilian owner, Marco, hurried over to greet them, hands outstretched, heavily-accented greetings falling from his lips. He waved them to a table in an alcove, returning seconds later to hand them menus.

Melanie sat into the seat with a sigh of relief. 'Bring us a bottle of that delicious Sicilian red wine we had the last time,' she said to him. 'A tempranillo, I think it was.'

'Ah, maybe the Viña Valoria?'

'That's the one, thanks.'

'You're drinking a lot more than you used to,' Caitlin commented, throwing her coat onto the back of an empty chair.

'A temporary crutch.' Melanie didn't tell her about getting hammered on whisky, that wasn't going to happen again. 'So much has been going on, it's an easy way to unwind.'

Caitlin leaned her elbows on the table and rested her chin on cupped hands. 'Have you given counselling some thought?'

Thought about it, done it, didn't like it. 'Are you hoping if you keep mentioning it, I'll eventually give in?' Melanie cocked her head but when her remark was met with silence, she added, 'I've thought about it.' The arrival of the wine interrupted any further comments.

Wine poured and their food order taken, Melanie sat back and tried to relax. It would be so much easier if she could tell Caitlin the whole truth, but it wasn't an option she wanted to take. 'These days my imagination runs away with itself all the time and paranoia seems to lurk around every corner, I think even a counsellor would find me difficult to sort out.'

Caitlin's expression softened and she stretched a hand across and laid it on Melanie's arm. 'You've been through a tough time, Mel. And no doubt, having the police calling around at three am didn't exactly help either.' Over dinner, as if determined to lighten the conversation, Caitlin talked about her new romance, a doctor she swore was the image of George Clooney. 'In his ER days, of course,' she insisted with a grin. 'And a body to die for too.'

'I suppose you did a full background check on him?'

Caitlin slurped a string of spaghetti. 'Of course, I know everything there is to know about him.'

It was the perfect opportunity. 'Did you get a chance to ask around about Liam Quinn?'

'Aha, that private investigator you asked me about. I didn't, not yet. Tell me, why are you so keen to find out about him? And don't give me any mumbo-jumbo about maybe needing to use him in some dim and distant future.'

Melanie couldn't tell her she'd already used Quinn's investigative services, nor could she voice her suspicions about his involvement in Hugo's death without telling her that she'd met Quinn in the pub. What a dreadfully tangled web she was spinning. Instead, she smiled and lied. 'Okay, you're right. I like the look of him. But I'm not risking my fingers being burned again.'

'Leave it with me,' Caitlin said, reaching out to pat her hand. 'I'll do a search on him, find out where he worked, see what his reputation was like. He could be what you need. Give me a day or two and I'll find out everything there is to know about him.'

The conversation turned to holiday plans, Caitlin's work, and general chat about life until the wine was gone and both were covering yawns. 'No stamina anymore,' Melanie said, putting her credit card down to pay the bill, insisting on it being her treat when Caitlin wanted to split it. 'I owe you this meal, at least.'

Marco had rung for taxis, one pulling up as they went out onto the street. 'You take this one,' Caitlin said, giving her friend a quick hug. 'You look like you're falling asleep on your feet.'

Melanie didn't argue, getting in and sinking onto the seat with a grateful smile.

'I'll let you know as soon as I hear anything, okay,' Caitlin said, shutting the door and waving as the taxi pulled away.

Traffic was heavy, barely moving at times. It would have been nice to shut her eyes, instead Melanie stared out the window at the pedestrians milling about and the neon lights of the city she loved. She felt as if she was in a state of suspended animation, waiting for something to happen, something she had no control over. It was unsettling. No, she needed to be honest with herself... it was terrifying.

The taxi had turned into Bloom Park Road before she noticed the flashing lights of a police car up ahead, her eyes widening when she realised it was outside her house. *What now?* The taxi pulled up behind it, the driver appearing totally unconcerned by the scene or her distress as she handed over the fare and clambered out.

The noise of her house alarm was deafening, the alarm box flashing blue in tandem with the lights of the police car. The two uniformed officers standing on her doorstep turned when she pushed open the gate. 'It's my apartment,' she said quickly, waving at it as if they might perhaps have misunderstood her.

One of them nodded. 'Your name?'

'Melanie Scott.' She reached into her bag and rummaged for something with her name on it to prove it was indeed her home, pulling out a bank statement and handing it over. Her initial frightened reaction had faded and she looked at her house, puzzled. There wasn't any window broken and the front door was still shut. 'It doesn't look as if there's anything wrong,' she said, taking the statement back.

'The alarm company contacted us,' the same officer said, as the other moved to peer in through the window. 'They insisted that both the door contact and a motion sensor had triggered an alarm but it looks pretty tight to me.'

Her alarm system was top of the range and she'd never had a problem. If any of the contacts on the door or windows were broken the monitoring company was automatically alerted, their policy in this situation being to send one of their staff to investigate. But if a motion sensor was triggered, they automatically involved the police. In the years she'd owned the apartment, the alarm had never gone off and she had it serviced every year. 'I'm really sorry,' she said, searching for her keys. 'I'm assuming there must be a fault of some sort.'

The officer reached for her keys. 'Best if we check inside. You have alarms on the rear windows?'

'Yes, but access from the back is very limited.'

Opening the door, both officers looked inside before waving her in. 'Perhaps you could silence the alarm.'

With the bell clanging in her head, she keyed in the four-digit code and sagged against the wall in the ensuing silence. Motioning her to stay where she was, the officers headed down the hallway and went from room to room. She heard them opening and shutting cupboards, relieved that they were being thorough.

Within a few minutes, they returned, their faces and posture relaxed. 'Everything looks satisfactory,' the one with the speaking part said. 'Perhaps you should have the alarm company in to service the system.' He resumed his stern manner to add, 'I must warn you, Ms Scott, two more false alarms and you're struck off our list.'

And with that, they gave a wave and left. She watched the car pulling away and went inside, locking the door, putting the safety chain on. Two of the lights on the alarm panel were flashing red; it indicated what the officers had told her, that the contacts on the front door had been broken and an internal motion sensor triggered. And yet there'd been no break in. She reset it, lost in thought.

Shrugging off her coat, she went into the bedroom and hung it up before heading to the kitchen. A whisky might have helped reduce the stress but, remembering the last time, she settled for tea, making a mug and bringing it through to the lounge. She sat and looked out of the French windows with a sigh. The view over the garden had lost its magic; her beautiful apartment no longer the oasis of calm it used to be. Hugo had spoiled it for her.

Self-pity shot through her, making her weak. She reached to put the mug of untouched tea on the low table beside her, freezing before completing the action. The table should have been clear, there shouldn't have been a sheet of white paper on it.

Putting the mug on the floor, she turned in her seat and looked at the paper. It was blank. At least on this side. She reached out and picked it up, carefully, delicately, by the edge as if afraid to contaminate or be contaminated by it, by whatever was written there. Because she knew something had to be. She brought it to her lap, flipped it over and dropped it, her eyes widening to see what was written.

Anne Edwards, it's time to do what Cherry did...

23

Melanie didn't know which frightened her the most, the message or the fact that someone had been inside her apartment, her home. A shiver shot through her and she wrapped her arms around herself in a desperate attempt to keep it together as the terrifying truth dawned... whoever was sending the emails had a key to her home. They could get in whenever they wanted.

The police officers had checked and found nothing wrong. They probably wouldn't rush back if her alarm went off again that night; they'd assume it was a fault. There was a safety chain on her door but a good bolt cutter would quickly deal with that.

It was impossible to stay there. She felt tears well and shook her head, there was no time to weep, she had to get out of there. But still she hesitated; the thought of leaving, of going out into the street suddenly frightened her more. What if they were waiting for her to do that? They would have known she'd find the note and might have anticipated her running away.

'Damned if I do, damned if I don't,' she muttered, still hugging herself. She thought about ringing Caitlin who would insist she went straight over. Melanie's reluctance wasn't down to the size of her friend's studio apartment, although it was seriously small, it was down to the repercussions. If she went, she'd have to tell Caitlin why she was there and reveal the sordid truth about her past. Melanie's lower lip trembled. Was it so wrong to want one part of her life free from the taint of what she had done?

But it was impossible to stay in her apartment knowing that someone had a key.

Fear blinded her. There seemed to be no way forward.

Was this the way it had gone for Cherry? Had she been so beaten down and defeated that the only solution lay in leaving it all behind? *As Matthew Thomas had done by the riverside all those years before.* Whoever had destroyed Cherry, was trying to destroy her; they were enacting the perfect revenge for his death.

But Melanie wasn't ready to give up yet. A spurt of anger blew a hole in the terror that surrounded her and suddenly she saw a solution. It was a stupidly simple one. She'd have the damn locks changed. It took only seconds using the internet to find a twenty-four-hour emergency locksmith. 'How soon can you come out?' she asked when she rang the number, giving a grin of relief when she was told within the hour.

In fact, it was forty minutes later that she heard a van pull up outside, peering through the shutters to check, breathing more easily when she saw the logo, *London Locks*. Without fuss or questions, the job was done in less than twenty minutes. The locksmith tested each of three keys before handing them to her. 'Don't forget,' he said, 'to replace any you've left with friends or key-holders.'

'Of course and thank you for the prompt service.' She shut the door behind him and turned with the new keys clinking in her hand. Three new ones to replace the three old. It took seconds to swop the one on her keyring. One spare should be here, in her bedside locker drawer, and one in the back of a drawer in her office. *Should be.* If her intruder had a key, they had to have obtained it from somewhere.

The drawer of her locker was filled with paraphernalia that had gathered over the years but she found the key lodged in a corner. She tossed it into the bin and replaced it with a new one. In the morning, she would check if the spare she'd left in her office was still there.

Even with the new locks, she didn't feel completely safe. That horrible detective, Burke, had taken the longest knife Melanie had, but she felt safer with something so she took a shorter one back to her room and shoved it under her pillow. To be even safer, she pulled the chest of drawers across the door. Then with a grunt of frustration, she pushed it back and went into the living room for the sheet of paper, taking it back to her room, replacing the chest of drawers.

The message on the page hadn't changed, the words still simple and stark. *Anne Edwards, it's time to do what Cherry did.* It was a message they could have sent by email; they'd chosen to deliver it as they had done simply to terrify her. And they'd succeeded.

She sat heavily on her bed. Poor Cherry, the job she loved had been destroyed by Facebook and Twitter trolls and the wicked graffiti daubed in the school and around Wethersham. Perhaps she'd received a similar message that had given her that final push. A dart of anger shot through Melanie. All these years living with the guilt of what she'd done, all these years listening to her mother's constant sniping and put-downs... she hadn't gone through all that only to give up now.

Taking the sheet of paper, she tucked it into the frame of a painting on the wall opposite her bed. It was the last thing she saw before she switched out the lights but now, instead of terrifying her, the words seemed to strengthen her resolve. Someone wanted her dead. They were going to have to do their own dirty work, she wasn't going to make it easy for them.

Surprisingly, she slept well, waking before her alarm went off. After a quick shower, she pinned her hair up. She wanted... no, she needed... to wear her favourite suit, the Armani she'd bought when she'd been promoted to senior associate three years before. It made her feel good, an armour of success and achievement. Classic, smart, it hadn't dated and provided the perfect façade to get her through the day.

With a final check in the mirror, she tugged her raincoat on over her suit and picked up her briefcase. She unlocked the front door, then hesitated with her hands on the safety chain. What if someone were waiting out in the street? Her fingers tightened on the door handle. What if they were at the station, waiting to push her under the tube? Trembling, she stepped backwards into the kitchen, sat onto a chair, and rested her head on her hand. 'Idiot,' she muttered, lifting her chin and gritting her teeth. Sadistic bastards. Were they watching and enjoying? Maybe she should get a taxi?

She couldn't live like this. Shaking her head, she stood and this time, set the alarm and left the house. She walked a bit faster, her eyes continuously darting around. On the platform, she stood back against the wall as she waited for the tube to arrive, only moving when the doors opened and the mass of people moved forward, joining in with them, feeling safer in the crowd.

The five-minute walk between the underground station and her office was busy with people rushing to work. Again, she stayed to the inside of the footpath, and never stopped scanning the bodies around her. It was with an overwhelming feeling of relief that she pushed open the door into the office, managing a shaky smile and greeting to Dan who, as usual, was standing in reception, his eyes automatically scanning every face that entered. Whoever wished her harm wouldn't get past him.

In the lift, she realised the stupidity of that thought. Whoever wished her harm could already be inside. She'd no idea who it was, so it could be anyone. When the lift stopped on the second floor, she got out and hurried the few steps to her office.

There was work to be done but she couldn't find any motivation to do it. Her hand reached for the desk phone and hovered over it before she pulled it back to take out her mobile and do a quick internet search. She dialled the number she found. 'I'd like to put my apartment on the market, it's on Bloom Park Road, Fulham. I want as quick a sale as possible even if it means dropping the price to get it.' Agreeing to meet the estate agent at her apartment the following night at seven, she hung up.

Next, she picked up the phone and rang Caitlin. Annoyingly, it went straight to voicemail. 'I wondered if you'd had a chance to look into Quinn yet.' Caitlin, she thought with a sad smile, would think that she was very eager to learn more about the man. How right she was.

Melanie settled down to work, feeling guilty she'd done so little. Several reports and innumerable emails later she sat back with a sigh, her eyes flicking to the door quickly when she heard a soft knock. 'Come in.'

'Morning,' Rona said, her stocky frame filling the doorway. 'I've the post sorted. There are a couple marked private that I haven't opened.' She put the pile of opened letters down first and the two unopened envelopes on top.

When the door closed behind her, Melanie reached for her post. The first envelope had Rabbie and Henderson's logo in one corner. Rona, she guessed, would have seen it too, and would be wondering why it was marked private rather than being looked after by her. Always curious about what was going on, she'd be more so now.

Shoving the letter in her bag to deal with at home, she reached for the second. No logo this time, a cheap brown envelope, handwritten name and address. No return address on the reverse. It wasn't unusual to get begging letters or ones asking for free advice so it was with little interest that she slipped a nail under the flap and slid it across to open. It contained one folded white sheet. Automatically, her heart rate increased and her mouth went dry as she reached in and withdrew it carefully, almost fearfully. What was that powder that could be sent through the post? Anthrax?

Putting it flat on the desk in front of her, she held her breath and opened it slowly. There was nothing inside. Letting her breath out, she looked at it. It was handwritten, a few lines and across the bottom in big curly writing, *Eric.*

Eric! She thought she'd seen the last of him, hadn't he told Quinn that he'd been trying to reassure her? She'd thought it strange at the time but had put him to the back of her mind, and now here he was again, jostling for a place at the front.

The letter was short and succinct.

Melanie, there has been enough pain. I owe you nothing but I'll give you something anyway. A word of warning. Be careful who you trust.

Apart from his swirly signature, that was it. He'd given her something all right, a huge headache. Be careful who you trust? Did he mean that she was trusting someone she shouldn't? Quinn?

She remembered watching Eric and Quinn together from her window. There'd been no rough stuff, Eric had even laughed before they'd walked away. Together. Almost friendly. Did they know each other? Did Eric know something about Quinn?

'Aargh,' she shrieked and quickly held a hand over her

mouth, hoping the sound hadn't travelled, her eyes glued to the door for long after she would have expected help to have come.

And then a worse thought hit her, sending her reeling backward, eyes wide, her hand clamping across her mouth to prevent another scream piercing the quiet. She was good at puzzles, sometimes it took her a while but generally she was good at working them out. Sometimes, you just needed enough pieces to be able to reach a solution. Eric's letter was the piece she had needed. Because if Liam Quinn knew him, mightn't it follow that he knew his brother, Matthew?

What Quinn had said about Hugo... that he wreaked havoc with people's lives... didn't that also apply to her? After all, she had destroyed so many lives: Matthew's, her mother's, her own, even Cherry's.

Another piece clicked into place. She'd left him here in her office alone. It had been the paperwork on her desk she'd been concerned about, relieved to find on her return that it hadn't been touched, that it looked as if Quinn hadn't moved during her absence. But maybe he had, maybe he'd made use of the opportunity she'd so stupidly handed him. He was a private investigator, after all, wasn't snooping their forte?

Her spare key! She hadn't looked for it yet. When she'd moved from the shared office, she'd simply taken the drawer holding yellow Post-its, boxes of paper clips, staples and elastic bands and swopped it for the empty one in her new office. She hadn't checked to see if the key was there and couldn't really remember the last time she'd seen it. With a jerk, she pulled the drawer open and searched among the mishmash of items, her scrabbling becoming more frantic with every second as the truth dawned. Then she slammed the drawer shut.

She was one hundred per cent sure. The key was gone.

Her face set in lines of anger.

Liam Quinn. How could she have been so wrong?

24

There had been something so solid and dependable about Quinn, Melanie had felt safe in his company. It made her squirm when she thought of it. Maybe she'd listen to Caitlin and go back to a counsellor when all this was sorted. A professional might be able to tell her why she continued to make such a mess of things. She pressed her lips together. She was not going to cry here; Rona could pop in at any time and there was a rumour that she reported any odd carry-on straight to the top.

Needing to get out of the office, even for a short while, she headed to the staffroom, hoping it would be empty. It was a comfortable, pleasant room, and at lunchtime there would be a constant trickle of people in and out but now it was quiet. The aroma of coffee filled the room; it tempted her to pour a mug she didn't really want. She sat with it cupped in her hands and heaved a sigh as a memory of Cherry popped into her head. Not the grown-up woman she'd never met but the child she'd known, full of laughter and hopes for a future that had been cut so short. Maybe it was a lesson Melanie needed to learn. There was only today, no promise of tomorrow. She needed to stop waiting around and act.

Picking up her mobile, she checked for a reply from Caitlin. Nothing. Tapping her thumb against the side of it, she thought about her next step. There didn't seem to be much choice. She needed to speak to Quinn… to confront him, with or without that background check. The easiest, and certainly safest way, was to have him call to the office. He didn't know about the letter from Eric and she'd given him no reason to believe she suspected him. She rang Rabbie and Henderson's to request an investigator. 'I used Liam Quinn the last time so if he were free, for continuity, it would be great if I could use him again.'

'No problem,' the administrator said quickly. 'Is this for an immediate start?'

'Yes, it's rather urgent.' Melanie wanted to talk to him today, while her tenuous grasp on courage lasted. 'It's not going to be for long though, a few hours' work. Today, if at all possible.'

'A few hours? Hmmm, okay, let me check and see what I can do.'

With her mobile pressed tightly to her ear, Melanie would swear she heard fingers flying over the keyboard, tap-tap-tapping to find the information she wanted. What if he were tied up on another job, unable to meet for days, weeks even? She couldn't stand many more days of this uncertainty, this fear, and she knew her courage would have deserted her by then. She'd been holding her breath, she let it out in a quiet hiss as the tapping continued for a few more seconds, then stopped.

'Yes, that's fine, Ms Scott, I've moved a few things about. I'll contact Liam and ask him to get in touch with you. That should be within an hour, okay?'

Within the hour. Couldn't be better. 'That's fine.' Melanie hung up and took the coffee back to her office. She sat sipping it, waiting for the phone to ring. It struck her that she should have asked for him to ring her mobile not the office phone. With the merger on hold, there wasn't any reason she should be employing an investigator. Rona was already viewing her with suspicious eyes and if she was, did that mean Richard and the other senior partners were too? She picked up her mobile to ring Rabbie and Henderson and request that Quinn ring her mobile when her desk phone rang. She was too late. 'A call from Liam Quinn for you,' Rona said, her voice cool. 'He says you're expecting it.'

Maybe Melanie was imagining the underlying note of curiosity, she kept her own voice cool and casual. 'Yes, that's fine, put him through, please.' She waited a beat, then as calm as she could, said, 'Hi, Liam. Thanks for getting back to me.'

She came to a quick decision; Rona was already suspicious and overly curious about what she was doing, having Liam come to the office would add fuel to that particular fire. Thinking on her feet, she said, 'There's some work I'd like to discuss with you. I did say it needed to be done immediately but something has come up since. Can we meet in the same place as last time, say at about six thirty?'

There was the merest whisper of a hesitation before he agreed to both time and location. 'I'll see you then,' he said and hung up.

Melanie replaced the receiver and sat back. The pub would be busy at six thirty, it would be a safe place to meet. What could he do to her in a room full of people? Now that she had the meeting arranged, she needed to think of a plan. Everything was still so very vague and hazy. Circumstantial, DI Elliot would probably have said and he'd have been right. She sighed. Maybe before the end of the day, Caitlin would get back to her with something she could use.

But the next phone call didn't give her the enlightenment she wanted; it wasn't even from Caitlin but from DI Elliot. 'I was thinking about you earlier,' she said when Rona put his call through, no mere hint of curiosity in her voice, it was rampant.

'In a good way, I hope?' Elliot said.

'Of course,' Melanie said without elaborating. 'Now, how can I help you?'

'I was wondering if you'd remembered who else you'd told about Hugo. I had a feeling you weren't being entirely honest with me.'

Melanie frowned and tapped her middle finger on the desk. Perhaps this was too good an opportunity to miss. 'Actually,' she said slowly, 'you're right, there was one other person.'

'Okay, and this person is?'

'You might even know him, Liam Quinn, he's ex-police, works now for Rabbie and Henderson, the private investigation service. I'm meeting him tonight to discuss some work I need him to do for me... about the merger,' she lied blithely. 'If you want to have a word with him, you could join us. We're meeting at The Fulham Arms, it's on the corner of Fulham and Cassidy Road.' Wouldn't that be the perfect safety net for her meeting with Quinn, for a policeman to arrive and if she were having a problem to save the day? 'I'm meeting him at seven thirty,' she said. That should give her enough time to speak to Quinn first.

There was silence as if Elliot were considering the wisdom of this. 'Yes, I might do that.'

Melanie mouthed a *yes*. 'Okay, I'll see you tonight,' she said and hung up.

She booked a taxi for five-thirty and tried to concentrate on getting some work done for the rest of the day, frequently losing focus as her mind drifted over the disaster her life had become. Hopefully, tonight she'd find a way to get through it.

At five-twenty, she stood and stretched. Time to go. She put on and belted her raincoat slowly while she considered whether to take her briefcase with her or not. All she needed was her purse and keys, and the coat had big pockets. She took out what she needed and shoved her briefcase under her desk. Down in reception, she waved a goodbye to the front-of-house staff as she walked through and gave the always-vigilant Dan a smile.

'You want me to check outside for you?' he said.

Startled, she turned to look at him. 'Sorry?'

'In case your ex is hanging around again.' Dan nodded towards the exit. 'You can't be too careful.'

He was being kind, wasn't he? *You can't be too careful.* Perhaps she'd imagined the emphasis that made it sound vaguely like a threat. She seemed to have lost her ability to judge. How could she with her history of being so easily fooled? 'That's not necessary,' she said sharply. She turned away without further comment, walked briskly to the door and pushed through.

Outside, her taxi was waiting; she climbed in, trying to put Dan's hurt expression from her mind. When she saw him next, she'd apologise. It wasn't his fault she was becoming paranoid. She dropped her head back on the headrest and shut her eyes, feeling the hot sting of tears. She didn't move until, almost an hour later, the taxi stopped outside The Fulham Arms.

It wasn't as busy as she'd expected. The table where they'd sat the last time was vacant and she took the seat Quinn had sat in then, facing the door, ready for him. She took off her coat and draped it over the chair to claim possession before heading to the bar. 'A mineral water, please.' She waited, her eyes flitting to the door, while the bartender filled her order and rang up the till. Quinn was late, she realised, handing over the money and taking her drink to the table.

It wasn't until six forty, that she saw him coming through, looking a little more dishevelled than last time, his face a little grey, patches of stubble on his chin from a quick or careless shave. She could feel her lips curving into a sneer; maybe guilt was getting to him.

'Sorry I'm late,' he said, reaching the table. He jerked his head towards the bar. 'I'll get a drink, you want anything?' He waited until she'd shaken her head before heading to where the lone bartender was pulling a pint for another customer.

Despite everything going round in her head all day, Melanie still had no idea how she was going to approach the conversation. When her mobile rang, she was tempted to ignore it, but a quick look told her it was Caitlin. Maybe it was the news Melanie had been waiting for? Quinn still hadn't been served. Keeping her eyes on him, she answered it. 'Caitlin, hi, you got my message?'

'Yes, sorry, it's been manic here today.'

Melanie saw Quinn give his order and knew she had only a couple of minutes. There was no time for chit-chat. 'Did you manage to find out anything for me?'

'A bit. He's got a nasty temper, your Liam Quinn. That's why he left the police. It wasn't his choice, Mel, he was thrown out. He's been in trouble since too, arrested for aggravated assault but not charged because surprise, surprise, the only witness vanished. I also have his school details but I doubt if they'll be of interest to you, and finally he's originally from Leeds. That's it.'

'Leeds,' Melanie squeaked. 'Are you sure?'

'That's what it says. Why, what's Leeds got to do with anything?'

Leeds. Where Matthew and Eric Thomas lived before the family moved to Wethersham. 'Nothing, just surprised, that's all.' Melanie watched the bartender place a pint on the counter. 'I have to go. Thanks, Caitlin, that was good timing. I'm having a drink with Quinn now.'

'What? Where are you?'

'We're in a pub. Sorry, have to go,' Melanie said and cut the connection, switching it off when it immediately rang again as she saw Quinn turn to come back. It was still only circumstantial rather than confirmation, but it was enough. She watched him cross the pub towards her, the pint in his hand. *The bastard.* She wanted to stand, take his pint and throw it at him, poke him in the eye with her manicured fingernails, slap him very hard across his smug face.

Instead, she watched while he settled into the seat opposite.

He took a long drink of his pint and put the glass down. 'Sorry again for being late, I've had a busy few days.' He smiled slightly, tilting his head to one side as he looked at her. 'To be honest, I only accepted this job because it was you.'

Yes, but not, as he was trying to insinuate, because he was attracted to her. She wasn't going to fall for that again. No, she knew why he wanted to take this job, maybe not the details – she didn't know what his connection was with Eric or Matthew – but armed with Caitlin's information, Melanie felt surer of her position. It was time to go in for the attack, aim for the jugular. His obvious exhaustion would, she decided, play in her favour.

'And why is that exactly?' She didn't know if it was the question itself, or the confrontational way she said it that made him sit back, eyes narrowing. 'Go on, tell me why you were so interested in seeing me again.' When he continued to sit staring at her, with a hard look in those grey eyes, she leaned towards him with a triumphant laugh. 'You can't, can you?' There was an edge of hysteria to the laugh, she bit it off and sat back.

He picked up his pint, drained it and waved the empty glass towards the bar, standing and moving away without a word. It gave her a few minutes to try to calm down. Now that she was here, it wasn't proving as easy as she'd expected to remain in control.

When he returned, he had a pint in one hand and a small

glass in the other. He put it on the table in front of her. 'Lagavulin, wasn't it?' he said, and took his seat.

She didn't want his damn drink, or to feel a smidgeon of pleasure that he'd remembered what she'd had the last time; nor did she want to feel grateful that he realised it was exactly what she needed.

'You look like you want to throw it at me,' he said. 'I'm not sure what I've done to make you feel like that but I would suggest, if you want to throw something, make it the water, if the price is anything to go by, Lagavulin is too good to throw away.'

His expression was one of amusement. Again, she wanted to slap him.

He must have seen the twitch in her hand or the anger on her face because he leaned forward, so suddenly as to startle a yelp from her. 'What the hell is going on?' he said, then sat back, his hands held up, palms outward. 'I'm sorry if I got the wrong end of the stick, okay? I get it. This is business only. That's fine with me.'

Without thinking, she reached for the glass and took a sip of the smoky whisky to steady her nerves. 'I know all about you,' she said, her voice low, trembling with emotion. 'I know what you've been doing.' She lifted her chin and tried to make her expression as fierce as she felt. 'You've failed. I'm stronger than Cherry was, you're going to have to do it yourself.'

He shook his head, reached for his glass and downed half the contents in one. Wiping a hand over his mouth, he looked at her with a closed expression. 'I have absolutely no idea what you're talking about, and I don't know anyone called Cherry.'

'Pah,' she spat out. 'And I suppose you don't know Eric Thomas either?'

Quinn blinked, looking puzzled. 'The man outside your office?' No wonder she'd been so easily fooled, Quinn was a very good actor. 'Yes, him, the man you were chatting to so amicably and who went with you without any fuss. I did wonder at the time why, but now I know. You know him.'

There was silence for a few minutes. She sipped her whisky and watched him, waiting for him to shrug in resignation, to acknowledge that his game was up. When he didn't, when he continued to sit frowning as if he really didn't know what was going on, she was goaded into saying more. 'I know it's been you sending those emails, and please don't bother lying.'

He shook his head.

'You admit it?'

Another shake. 'I don't know what bee you have in your bonnet,' Quinn said slowly, 'but something seems to be terribly wrong here. I'm just not sure what it is. You seem to believe I'm involved in something dodgy. I'm not, but I'm too tired to waste my energy arguing. I came because I foolishly thought you'd felt the same attraction as I did the last time we met.' He gave a short laugh. 'I thought that was why you'd asked for me specifically. Now,' he said, checking his watch, 'if you'd like to tell me the details of the job, I can get home.'

'There's no damn job,' she snarled. 'And you can't go, the police want to speak to you. They're coming here at seven thirty.'

'The police? Why do they want to speak to me?'

This wasn't working out at all how Melanie had planned. He didn't look the slightest bit guilty for what he'd put her through. In fact, she thought looking at him closely, he looked fed up and vaguely irritated. 'Hugo Field was murdered. Stabbed.'

'Hugo Field? The man you told me about?' Quinn's frown deepened. 'Why do they want to speak to me? I didn't know the man. I've never met him.'

'They want to speak to you because I told you about what he'd done... stealing that information from me. What was it you called it... catfishing?'

He stared at her. 'Please, don't tell me they think I'm some kind of vigilante, that I killed him out of some idea of vengeance?' When she said nothing, he groaned. 'Seriously? I felt sorry for what you'd gone through but I barely know you and, believe it or not, I'm not a violent person.'

'That's not what I've been told.'

Quinn drained his pint and put the glass down with a snap. 'I don't know who you've been talking to, but if they said I was the violent sort, they were lying.'

'Yes, well, funnily enough, I prefer to believe her not you, and thanks to Caitlin, I know all about you. That you're from Leeds, that you were thrown out of the police force. I know every damn thing.'

Shaking his head, he stood and looked down at her, his voice cold. 'I've never been to Leeds; I left the police force because I found I could make more money in the private sector. Whatever else you've heard, that's the truth. Now, if the police want to speak to me, tell them to contact me, I'm not hanging around.' He walked away without another word.

'I'll ask Eric, he'll tell me the truth about you,' she said loudly, causing him to stop, turn and glare at her. She flinched, feeling a dart of fear that faded as he shook his head and left the pub. She sat back, ignoring the eyes turned her way, the whispers. Nothing had gone as planned. Now, not only had she no proof that he was responsible for what was going on, but she'd put him on his guard.

It was almost seven thirty. She'd wait for DI Elliot and tell him everything, about Wethersham, her hand in Matthew's death, the emails, every damn thing.

Decision made, she sat and waited but at seven forty-five, with the pub filling around her and the noise levels high, she decided it was time to leave. It seemed not even DI Elliot could be trusted.

She stumbled from the pub, forgetting she'd planned to ring

for a taxi until she was several yards away. Looking around the empty street, she walked more quickly, breaking into a jog, then a run as she rounded the corner into Bloom Park Road. Her kitten heels weren't designed for speed, she slipped and would have gone over on her ankle if she hadn't reached for the wall to prevent her fall, her breath coming in noisy gasps. There was nobody around, the street quiet, deserted. Or was Quinn hiding somewhere, waiting for her? She kicked her shoes off, left them there and ran to her apartment.

25

Inside, Melanie whimpered as she put the safety chain in place and backed away from the door. The evening had been an absolute disaster. 'A disaster, an absolute fucking disaster.' She didn't normally swear but her nerves were frayed.

She switched on all the lights as she passed and went into the kitchen where she pulled off her coat and threw it over the back of a chair. 'An absolute disaster.' Every time she thought there was light at the end of the tunnel, the stupid tunnel branched off and she was left in darkness all over again. She stood, staring across the room, unable to think. The kitchen door was open and it was several seconds before she processed what she was seeing on the floor of the hall. Blood was smeared along the pale wooden floor.

Terror sent her heart thumping. Blood... bloody steps... Groaning, she looked down at her feet, lifting one, then the other. Her tights had been shredded in the short run from where she'd kicked off her shoes and somewhere, she'd walked on something sharp. She hadn't felt anything and it wasn't painful now but blood was oozing from a deep cut on the sole of her right foot. The bloody footsteps were hers.

It seemed to be the final straw; she sat and started to cry, the hopeless, forlorn cry of someone who has reached the end of their tether.

Minutes later, the ringing of the house phone broke through her sobs. Her mobile was still switched off, she guessed it was Caitlin ringing to ask what happened with Quinn. Snuffling, she stood, and using her left foot and the heel of her right, she hobbled across to pick it up.

'Hello,' she said, trying to instil some strength into the one word. 'Hello.' Less strong this time and when there was still no answer, any attempt at bravery vanished. 'Leave me alone,' she shrieked into the receiver and dropped it on its cradle, backing away from it, hoping with every breath left in her that it wouldn't ring again.

When it didn't, she almost sobbed with relief and limped to the kitchen to search for a dressing for her foot. She found one and sat to apply it to the wound but when she saw the dirt on her feet, she groaned, stood and made her way slowly to the bathroom. A shower would have been the ideal solution but it was a noisy electric one, she wouldn't be able to hear if anyone tried to break in. She gulped at the thought of being so vulnerable. Instead, she sat on the edge of the bath, quickly washed and dried her feet and applied the dressing to the cut. She used the damp towel to wipe the bloodstains from the hall and kitchen floor, threw it into the washing machine, then sat and wondered what she was going to do.

If she didn't choose to end her own life, would Quinn arrange an accident? Maybe he'd lie in wait for her in a week or two when her guard had dropped. It would probably be easy for him, Caitlin said he was no stranger to violence. Opening her bag, Melanie took out her mobile and switched it on. Three messages from Caitlin, each more frantic than the next, wanting to know about Quinn.

Melanie's phone battery was running low. She reached for the house phone and dialled Caitlin's number from memory. 'Hi,' she said, when it was answered almost immediately.

'Melanie, you dark horse,' Caitlin said. 'Out with Liam Quinn!'

'He rang and asked me out for a drink,' Melanie lied. 'I thought I might as well go, see what he was like away from work.'

'And then I go and spoil it for you with that information. I am sorry.'

Melanie sighed. 'It doesn't matter, I won't be seeing him again.'

There was silence for a few seconds, then Caitlin's voice, quieter, more sympathetic. 'You won't? Oh no, is that because of what I told you?'

'To some extent, but it was more that we didn't seem to have much in common.' Melanie yawned loudly, hoping her friend would get the message.

'You sounded a bit odd earlier when I spoke to you. Are you sure you're okay?'

Melanie was far from okay, her life was a maelstrom from which she seemed unable to escape. 'I'm fine, just tired, Caitlin. It's been a stressful few days.'

'Of course it has. If you're sure you're all right and since you've no juicy gossip, I'll let you get your beauty sleep.'

'Okay, goodnight, talk soon.' Relieved to have been let off so easily, Melanie sat back. What to do now? She couldn't wait around to see what was going to happen. Perhaps she should go to the police. She was sure Quinn was responsible not only for Hugo's death but indirectly for Cherry's and for the campaign of intimidation against herself. Unfortunately, she had no facts, nothing concrete at all, and as DI Elliot had said, they dealt with facts, not emotions. She could imagine Elliot, his garish tie swinging as he insisted it was all circumstantial.

But Eric had warned her against Quinn, so he must know something. She'd told Quinn she'd speak to Eric and ask him. It had been an empty threat but maybe that was exactly what she should do. Speak to him, get him to admit that it was Quinn that he'd warned her against trusting and find out exactly what he knew.

Then she'd go to DI Elliot.

A decision made, of any sort, gave her some consolation. She was going to *do* something. When the house phone rang, she gasped, holding her breath, releasing it on a shake of her head. It would be Caitlin having forgotten to tell her something. Melanie picked it up. 'Hello.'

Nothing. But the line wasn't dead. Pressing the phone close to her ear, she was sure she could hear a faint inhale and exhale. 'Hello?' The sound she heard increased in volume. A deep, heavy gulp of air and a long hissing release sound. She dropped the handset back into its cradle and stepped away, shaking her head as she moved. 'Bastard,' she said to it, backing from the room.

All the lights were still on, the front door a full stop at the end of the startlingly bright hall. She'd leave all the lights on, go to bed and burrow under the duvet. It was a good plan, and she'd taken a step towards her bedroom when she was stopped by a faint, unidentifiable sound. It seemed to be coming from the front door. A rustling sound. Leaves blown against it by the wind, perhaps. She stood staring, willing the noise to stop but it didn't, instead it grew louder, the rustle changing to a rattle, then to a banging. Someone was outside the door. Quinn? He knew where she lived. So did Eric Thomas.

She cried out when she heard a new sound. The scratching, scraping sound of metal on metal. Someone was trying to put a key into the lock. It wouldn't fit, would it? Despite the new lock and the keys all safely in her possession, she half-expected the door to open and push against the safety chain. She imagined long fingers creeping around the door frame, fingers strong enough to grab hold of the chain and pull it from the wall, then he'd be inside and vengeance, at last, would be his.

With her imagination in overdrive and her breath hitching noisily as she imagined those ghastly fingers closing around her neck, it was a few minutes before she realised the sounds had stopped. She held her breath, her hand pressed over her mouth and listened to the heavy, thick, unfriendly silence. She knew, whoever it was, Quinn or someone else, they were on the other side of the door, waiting.

Slowly, her eyes still fixed on the door, she backed up, slipped into the bedroom and shut the door quietly. It wasn't until she'd pulled the chest of drawers across that she let her breath out in a shuddering sigh. She lay on the bed and pulled the duvet up over her head. In the dark warmth, she told herself that she was stronger than Cherry.

Melanie covered her mouth with a corner of the duvet so that anyone listening couldn't hear her sob.

26

Melanie slept fitfully, waking at every real and imagined creak and squeak, throwing off the duvet and her robe during the night, too hot, too trapped. Finally, when the first light of day crept around the sides of the curtains, she swung her feet to the floor and winced as she put pressure on her damaged foot. She twisted it around to see. The dressing had come off during the night but it was no longer bleeding; she'd live.

It was easier to be brave in the morning; she pulled on her robe, shoved the chest of drawers out of the way and opened the door to look down the hall. Her imagination had really got the better of her the night before. There'd been nobody there. Of course there hadn't. To convince herself, she took the safety chain off and opened the front door. It was a bright, if chilly, morning. Nothing out of the ordinary. She was about to shut it when she noticed scratches on the shiny new lock. It hadn't been her imagination at all, someone had tried to get in. Someone who didn't care that she was there, who didn't see her as a threat.

Or had it been a deliberate attempt to frighten her? If that had been the reason, it had achieved its aim. She slammed the door shut so hard the sound reverberated through the apartment and followed her into the kitchen. She needed coffee.

While the kettle boiled, she had a quick shower. Fifteen minutes later, dressed for work, she sat in the kitchen with a mug cradled between her hands.

If she spoke to Eric could she persuade him to tell her the truth?

It didn't seem like she'd anything to lose.

She rang for a taxi to take her to the office; there were too many places between her apartment and the station where she was vulnerable, narrow walkways and overgrown gardens where someone could hide, ready to pounce or drag her inside. The station itself heaved with danger. A taxi from her door to the door of Masters would be slower, but safer.

It arrived on time, tooting its horn when she didn't immediately open the door. Setting her alarm, she locked up and dashed the short distance to the taxi and wrenched open the door. She tumbled inside, drawing a stare from the driver which she ignored as she looked up and down the street as far as she could see. There was nobody lurking, the street looked empty. But there were so many places someone could hide, how did she really know?

Paranoia was making her irritable, restless, and incredibly jumpy. When the taxi was stopped in traffic or at lights, she shut her eyes, afraid to see a leering ghoulish face at the window. No matter how many times she told herself she was being stupid she couldn't seem to regain any equilibrium.

Outside her office building, she paid the fare and hesitated with her hand on the handle before pushing it open and walking straight-backed and tunnel-visioned to the door, taking the broad steps at a run. In the reception lobby, feeling safe, she looked around for Dan. She owed him an apology for the way she'd spoken to him the day before. To her surprise, he wasn't there, instead a security man whose name she didn't know gave her a once-over before directing his attention back to the door.

Approaching the reception desk, she smiled a hello at Petra, their front-of-house manager. 'Dan on a day off?'

'No, he rang in sick. Tummy bug or something,' she said. One overplucked eyebrow rose almost to her hairline as she reached out with long, brightly-coloured nails for her keyboard.

Tummy bug? Melanie had worked for Masters coming up to seven years and she couldn't remember a day when Dan hadn't been there. There seemed to be so little in her life she could depend on; his absence, innocent though it may be, unsettled her. She was even more unsettled when she examined her thoughts. *Innocent though it may be.* Did she really think Dan's absence was suspicious?

Maybe she'd been right and his words the other day had held a threat. She felt the strands of paranoia tighten. In her office, she sat and stared at the wall. *Dan?* She shook her head. Ridiculous. She'd known the guy for years. Dan had always seemed to be one of the good guys... but hadn't she thought the same of Quinn?

She was going around in circles. She'd speak to Eric, find out what he knew about Quinn and go from there.

Decision made, she rang the car showroom but although she tried several times, each time it went to answerphone. What kind of a car showroom didn't have someone to answer the phone? She tapped her fingers on the desk in frustration. Now that she'd made the decision, she didn't want to put off speaking to him. Picking up her desk phone, she ordered a taxi, then pressed the number for Rona's phone. 'I'm going to be gone for the rest of the day,' Melanie said. 'Any problems, you can email me, okay?' She half-expected to be quizzed on where she was going so was pleasantly surprised when the reply was an unconcerned, *That's fine.*

Minutes later she was on her way back to Edgware Motors. It was a long, uncomfortable journey, heavy traffic forcing the taxi to continuously stop and start. Her earlier fear hadn't receded. She kept her eyes shut, rested her head back and tried to get things straight. If Eric confirmed her fears about Quinn, she'd ring Elliot... then it would be all over, wouldn't it?

'Looks like you won't be buying a car today, love,' the taxi driver said, after almost an hour's jerky, unpleasant drive.

She leaned forward to peer out the front windscreen, her eyes widening at the police cars and ambulance parked on the roadside.

'This is as close as I can get you.' The taxi stopped several yards from a crowd that had gathered, some with craned necks trying to see what was going on, others with arms wrapped around each other and tearful, shocked faces.

'This is fine,' Melanie said, paying the fare and climbing out.

Now she knew why the phone wasn't being answered, there'd been a robbery or something. Joining the edge of the crowd, she looked around in frustration, trying to find Eric. He wasn't in the group that was kept back from the door by crime-scene tape and two burly, uniformed police officers, but there was someone among them she recognised. The woman with the pink hair, standing hunched over, a picture of misery.

Melanie edged through the gawking bystanders to her side. 'Hello,' she said, then repeated the word a little louder until she got the woman's attention. 'Has there been a robbery?' The woman showed no recognition, staring at Melanie with blank, red-rimmed eyes. 'I met you here on Saturday, remember, I'm a friend of Eric's.'

The woman's creased face seemed to fold in on itself, then she opened her mouth and wailed. It was a ghastly sound, full of sorrow and disbelief. Horrified, Melanie put an arm around her shoulder and led her away from the crowd to an area around the corner of the building that was sheltered and quiet.

'Please stop,' Melanie said as the wailing continued unabated. 'You'll make yourself sick.' Reaching into her pocket, she pulled out a clean tissue and pressed it into the woman's hand. 'Come on, stop crying.'

The woman's pink, tear-blotched face now matched her hair. She gave a heaving snuffle, blew her nose noisily and wiped her tears away with the arm of her coat. 'You still don't know, do you?'

The feeling of dread was instant. 'Tell me.'

'Eric. He was found dead in the doorway this morning. It was his turn to open the showroom, you see, so he was here first. One of the other lads, Vic, found him lying in a pool of blood. Eric's bunch of keys were in the door but he'd never managed to open it.'

Dead. Melanie felt suddenly weak and nauseous. She wrapped her arms around her stomach, trying to hold herself together. The last thing she'd said to Quinn... *I'll ask Eric, he'll tell me the truth about you.* My God, had she signed the man's death warrant?

27

Melanie gave the woman a hug. 'I have to go. Will you be okay?'

'I'll never be okay again,' the pink-haired woman said, her shattered expression saying clearly that Eric had been much more to her than simply a co-worker. She patted Melanie's arm and headed back to the group that congregated outside the police cordon.

Eric was dead. Melanie stumbled back to the road. There were police cars and policemen standing about but she couldn't gather the courage to speak to them. She'd get a taxi, go straight to the police station, and talk to DI Elliot. But no magic worked in her favour and no taxi suddenly appeared. Feeling exposed, she looked across the road towards The Londoner, the pub where she'd met Eric only days before. It would be safer inside than standing there.

The lunchtime crowd had already started to gather and the only table free was the same table in the window where she'd sat with Eric. It gave her an eerie sensation to sit there, looking across the road to where he'd been killed. She dragged her eyes away and reached into her bag for her mobile. The card DI

Elliot had given her was tucked into a side pocket, she slid it out and quickly dialled the number, relieved to immediately hear his calm voice. 'Detective Inspector Elliot.'

'It's Melanie Scott.' Her words rushed out on an exhaled breath. 'I need to speak to you, to tell you everything.'

'Okay.' He dragged the word out. 'Where are you?'

'In a pub, The Londoner, in Edgware.' She wondered if he thought she spent her time in pubs. The Fulham Arms last night, The Londoner today. Then she remembered, he hadn't turned up. 'You never came last night,' she blurted out.

'No,' he said. 'Listen, stay where you are, I'll be with you in about an hour, okay?'

Get across the city in an hour? Impossible. She resigned herself to a long wait. Leaving her coat across the back of the chair, she went to the bar and ordered coffee. She still felt nauseous and weak but the list of sandwiches on a board behind the bar looked appetising. Maybe she'd feel better if she ate something. Certainly, she couldn't feel any worse.

Her order given, she sat back in the chair; her eyes fixed on the drama across the road. The crowd around the front door was thinning, probably bored from staring at the sides of the white tent that had been erected around the crime scene. A breeze had picked up, and the loose ends of the bright yellow-and-black crime-scene tape that had kept the crowd at a distance fluttered almost gaily. There was nothing to see, but she couldn't drag her eyes away.

The pub was either very busy or they were short-staffed because it was fifteen minutes before a harried woman came towards her with a tray bearing coffee and the chicken sandwich Melanie had ordered. The coffee was good, if not as hot as she liked, and the sandwich was perfect. It was gone within minutes and she sat back sipping her now-cold coffee and resumed her stare across the street.

To her surprise, a little over twenty minutes later the door opened and DI Elliot walked into the pub, a brown, scruffy raincoat open over his suit. From across the room, she could see he was wearing yet another ghastly tie, this one a neon orange that stood out for all the wrong reasons. His eyes scanned the room, zoning in on her as she raised a hand to attract his attention.

He made his way through the crowded pub and folded his gangly frame into the seat opposite. 'You have a bird's eye view,' he said, looking out the window.

'You know about it?'

He smiled briefly. 'We haven't yet got that blasé about murders that we don't know about each one. A colleague is heading the investigation, I called over and had a few words with him before coming here. I'm not actively involved in it though.' His eyes narrowed as he looked at her. 'At least, I'm not yet. I wouldn't be a very good detective if I didn't think, bizarrely, that there might be a link between the dead man, your presence here and your panicky call to me.'

Her gaze flicked between him and the fluttering crime-scene tape, finally settling on him. It was time to tell her tale. 'This is quite a story,' she said, 'you might want to get something to drink or eat.'

'Coffee,' he said, and looking at her empty cup, asked, 'Some more for you?'

'An Americano, please.'

He returned a few minutes later and placed the coffee on the table in front of her. 'Okay,' he said, 'fire ahead.'

She took a sip of her coffee, good and hot this time, and wondered where to begin. 'It's probably best if I start at the beginning,' she said, almost to herself. Taking occasional sips of coffee, over the next twenty minutes – sometimes having to go back to clarify something and sometimes stopping when her voice choked with emotion – she told him everything. He was a good audience: he didn't interrupt, didn't even feel the need to make noncommittal sounds; he sat and listened, his expression carefully neutral. But his eyes, she noticed as she stumbled over her words for the umpteenth time, stayed warm and encouraging.

'...so, I came today to ask Eric to confirm that he knows Liam Quinn and to ask what his connection was to Matthew.' She looked out the window towards the showroom. 'But as you know I was too late. Worse,' she said, her voice breaking, 'it's my fault. If I hadn't told Quinn that I was going to ask him, Eric would still be alive.'

'These emails you got, can I see them?'

'Of course.' Melanie picked up her phone, scrolled through and handed it to him, watching his face as he read, feeling a little uneasy at his lack of response. 'You do believe me, don't you?'

Ignoring her question, he returned her phone. 'And you think this ex-policeman, Liam Quinn, is responsible for these and for breaking into your home? All to get revenge for the death of this Matthew Thomas?'

She nodded, too emphatically. 'I know it all sounds so far-fetched. But don't they say revenge is a dish best served cold? Someone waited until Cherry and I had made it to the top of our careers before they decided it was time to make us pay. Cherry paid with her life; I'm not willing to do the same.' She frowned. 'You should have come last night, as you promised you would, you could have asked him questions then.' And maybe, she wouldn't have blurted out about speaking with Eric and maybe he'd still be alive. Turning away from him to hide the tears that had welled, she looked out the window.

'I didn't promise I'd come,' he said calmly, 'and, to be honest, I don't think anything you or I could have done would have changed the outcome here. My colleague told me that there was no attempt made to enter the showroom and Eric's wallet was still in his pocket so theft doesn't appear to have been the motive. They are running with the theory that he was targeted for some reason but if that's the case it was planned in advance by someone who knew he'd be opening the showroom today.'

She turned back to look at him, her eyes brighter, feeling pathetically grateful. 'Really?'

'Really. If Quinn is involved with his murder, and' – Elliot shook his head – 'nothing you've said so far is convincing me of this, he would have had to have planned it long before last night.'

Relief swept through her. She'd been responsible for one person's death; she hadn't wanted to be responsible for another. 'Thank you,' she said. She saw him nod, then smooth a hand down his tie. 'What are you thinking?' She smiled at his look of surprise. 'You do that,' she said, pointing to his tie. 'You rub your hand down it when you're going to come out with something I won't like. At least' – she shrugged – 'that's how I've been interpreting it.'

He flicked the end of his tie. 'A bit like worry beads, I suppose.' He sighed. 'It can't have been easy for you, all these years, keeping your secret. And these emails you've been getting... it's obvious they've had a bad effect on you. Then to cap it all, you fell into the hands of a scam artist like Hugo.' Elliot smiled sympathetically. 'Now I think you're seeing monsters where there are only ordinary people.'

She bit back a groan of frustration. He thought she was paranoid. It was what she'd thought herself, more than once, so she shouldn't be surprised. 'It was the comment he made about men like Hugo wreaking havoc with people's lives without ever being brought to justice. Now that you know my story, couldn't that also apply to me?' She leaned forward slightly, willing him to agree. 'And there was definitely something between Quinn and

Eric.' She met his calm gaze. 'You think I'm being paranoid, but I know I'm right.' She sat back and stared out the window to where she'd last seen Eric ambling back to the showroom. 'If only I'd managed to speak to Eric. It's why I was coming here. To see him, to get him to name names rather than give me that stupidly vague warning about not trusting people.' Dropping her hands on the table, she said more quietly, 'I mean, what was that all about? Why couldn't he have simply said "don't trust Quinn?"'

'Maybe it isn't who he meant.'

She took a deep breath and let it out in a gust of frustration and confusion. There was no point in continuing to argue, she knew she was right but with Eric dead she'd no way of proving it. 'You will look into him though, won't you?' she said, more calmly.

'Yes, and I'll keep you in the loop, don't worry.' He smiled, looking suddenly much younger. 'Don't tell DI Ballantyne that I'm being so unprofessional.'

'Caitlin would understand.' Melanie leaned closer again, her eyes entreating. 'She doesn't know about Anne Edwards. I've never told her.' She saw his surprised look and shook her head. 'I wanted a part of my life to be... unsullied, I suppose, by what I'd done as a child. Caitlin thinks I'm this honest, hard-working strait-laced lawyer, I'd like her to stay thinking that of me. Is that possible?'

'There'd be no reason for DI Ballantyne to read City of London police reports.' A group of people at the next table stood to leave, shouting loud goodbyes across to the bar staff, banging chairs, laughing loudly, filling the air with cheerful sounds that hung heavily over the two by the window. When the group had left and relative silence resumed, Elliot looked at Melanie kindly. 'Listen, don't worry. I appreciate you telling me your story, and I know you believe Liam Quinn is to blame for everything but' – he shook his head – 'leave the detective work to me. I will look into him, don't worry, but nothing you've said has given me reason to look at him too closely.' He moved his hand as if to rub it down his tie, stopping with a smile. 'Hmmm, I'll need to stop doing that.' A serious expression returned. 'I won't be writing anything about what you've told me yet. You haven't broken any laws by changing your name, after all.' He tilted his head questioningly. 'You haven't, have you?'

She smiled at his suddenly worried expression. 'No, relax, I had it legally changed by deed poll years ago.'

'Good.' He looked at his watch. 'Bloody hell. I have to fly.' He reached out and patted her hand gently. 'Go home, stay safe. You have my number, ring me any time, okay?'

She smiled gratefully and watched him go with regret. She felt safe in his company. The thought made her frown.

Hadn't she felt the same about Liam Quinn?

28

Melanie sat for a few minutes after Elliot's departure, reluctant to leave a place where she felt safe. Or maybe she was simply afraid to go home. But she had to, she realised with a frustrated shake of her head, the estate agent was coming around to do a valuation at seven. There was no point in sitting there until then, she needed to get home to make the place look respectable.

Ringing for a taxi, she sat back and stared out the window. Eric Thomas, he hadn't been very pleasant to talk to but she supposed it was understandable. She wondered if his parents were still alive. Now they'd lost both their sons... and despite what DI Elliot had said, she couldn't entirely shake the feeling that somehow, she'd been to blame.

She waited until the taxi pulled up outside before grabbing her coat and bag and hurrying from the pub. A light rain had started to fall. It was only early afternoon, but low, dark clouds made it feel later. By the time the taxi pulled into her street, the rain had turned into a deluge. A loud crack of thunder rumbled in the distance followed seconds later by a fork of lightning across the darkened sky. She shivered as she handed the driver the fare.

'It's a bad 'un,' he said. 'You better run for it.'

Run she did, but her wet fingers slipped on the gate handle and fumbled with the keys as she tried to get one in the lock. Cursing her clumsiness, she pushed the door open, stepped inside and shook herself, drops flying everywhere.

Another louder crash of thunder made her turn quickly and shut the door.

She was by nature an organised person, so the apartment just needed a quick tidy to make it ready for the agent. It didn't take long and checking the time, she saw it was only four. She checked her phone for emails; nothing from the office, nothing further from *nobody*. She frowned; the note left on the table had been the last contact. Two days ago. Was this another form of intimidation, keeping her wondering, on edge, bloody terrified?

She'd have liked coffee but she was jittery enough and settled for camomile tea, hoping it would calm her, but pretty sure it hadn't a chance. Her apartment had lost its gloss, even sitting looking out the French windows to the garden no longer had the power to calm or charm. It was all spoiled for her. Maybe she'd look a bit further from the city, she'd get more for her money, perhaps even a house. She looked out at the dripping foliage, the dark clouds that loomed across the sky and thought briefly about moving somewhere sunny.

Tempting, but she'd never leave London.

She put her mug down as she felt weariness sweep over her. So terribly tired, so utterly exhausted. She rested her head back, shut her eyes and fell into a light doze, her jaw relaxing so that her mouth opened a little, drool puddling to the side of her mouth. A noise woke her. She sat up and tried to shake away that brief disorientation that comes with sleeping in the wrong place at an odd time. What had she heard? Her eyes swept the room, peering out into the garden where daylight was fading fast; shadows, dense darkness, the flicker of movement. Wind perhaps, tossing the wet leaves? Nothing more threatening than that; the garden was safe. She gulped, wiped her mouth, and jumped up to pull the curtains.

The sound came again, louder, more insistent... recognisable. It was nothing more sinister than the doorbell. The clock on the wall told her she'd slept for nearly an hour. It was too early for the agent and she wasn't expecting anyone else. She moved into the hall, feeling a flicker of fear when she realised she'd left the safety chain off. Slow steps took her to the door, her hand reaching out for the chain to slide it into place, the chain rattling against the door, the noise swallowed by the sound of her heart thumping.

'Melanie?'

'Caitlin?' Stepping closer to the door, Melanie held her ear against the wood. 'Caitlin, is that you?'

'Of course it's me, you muppet, open the door before I drown.'

Relief vied with confusion as she unhooked the chain, turned the latch and pulled open the door. 'Caitlin, thank goodness it's you.' Melanie stood back to let her inside. 'You scared me, why didn't you ring to tell me you were coming. Anyway,' she said, her forehead creasing in puzzlement, 'how did you know I'd be here?'

Caitlin walked over to the landline. 'I have been ringing. I tried your mobile and there was no answer so I tried your landline and it was dead.' She picked up the handset and set it back onto its cradle firmly. 'It wasn't in place; the battery's gone flat.'

Melanie hadn't heard her mobile ring but the bar had been noisy and although she'd checked for emails, she hadn't thought to check for missed calls. 'Sorry,' she said, with a shake of her head, 'it's been one of those days.'

Caitlin flopped onto the sofa. 'I rang your office and Rona said you'd come home so I thought I'd call and see how you were.'

Melanie frowned briefly, then shook her head on a sigh. 'I was tired so decided to give myself the afternoon off.'

'I'm not surprised, you've had a tough time of it recently.' Caitlin stood and went to Melanie, putting her arm around her shoulder and pulling her into a quick hug. 'I'm glad you're okay, I was worried about you.'

It was comforting to have someone to care, Melanie stayed there for a few seconds, wishing life was always this simple. She felt her friend's warm breath on her cheek, felt soothed by the strength of her touch. Not for the first time, she wished she could tell her the truth, wished she could be sure that their friendship would survive it. She pulled away. 'I have some bad news.'

Caitlin frowned and moved backward to sit on the edge of the sofa. 'Tell me?'

Melanie could leave out the bit about Eric Thomas and tell her everything else. 'I think Quinn might be involved in Hugo's murder.'

'Liam Quinn? Seriously?' Caitlin's eyes widened. 'Of course, he did work for Masters too. He must have heard about the merger and decided to make some money. So, what was it? A falling out of thieves?'

Melanie stopped her jaw dropping open with effort. She had been so fixated on the idea of Quinn as a vigilante, she'd not given a thought to him being involved in the insider trading. Money, it was always at the bottom of things. 'It looks like it,' she said, unwilling to admit she'd not given that idea consideration.

'Hugo and now Quinn. You've not had much luck recently,' Caitlin said. 'Do you think Quinn was responsible for sending the emails to you too?'

'Yes, I do.' Melanie stood abruptly. 'It's all coming together at last. How about I make us a cup of tea?' She moved towards the doorway. 'Sit and relax, I'll only be a minute.'

Melanie willed her feet to carry her forward without stumbling. Keeping the smile in place with difficulty, she edged from the room and into the kitchen where she noisily filled the kettle and switched it on before looking around for her phone. Her handbag was hanging from a chairback. 'Just be a minute,' she sang out, hurrying to grab it, her fingers rummaging inside for her phone, afraid to take her eyes off the doorway.

'Okay?' Caitlin suddenly appeared, a strange look on her face.

'Yes, I thought I heard my phone ring,' Melanie said with an attempt at a laugh. 'There's so much junk in my bag, it's hard to find anything inside.'

'Let me,' Caitlin said, snatching the bag from her hand. She pulled the phone out and threw it across the room. 'I shouldn't have mentioned the damn emails, should I?' she said, shaking her head. 'And I was being so careful.'

Melanie pulled a chair out and sat heavily, her head spinning. The thoughts that were running through her head were impossible. Caitlin was her friend, she trusted her completely. Melanie looked up at her, saw the hard look in her eyes, the twist of her mouth. 'You also shouldn't have said Rona told you I'd come home. I hadn't told her where I was going.'

29

'Tut, tut, I'm really off my game today.' Caitlin leaned against the kitchen counter, arms crossed, waiting.

She didn't have to wait long. Melanie shook her head, a lump in her throat. 'I don't understand.'

'You really are the stupidest, most gullible person I've ever had the misfortune to meet.'

'We were friends!'

A sneer cocked one edge of Caitlin's mouth. 'No, we were never friends. I know who you are, Anne Edwards.'

Melanie felt her world shatter.

Caitlin's sneer grew uglier. 'Eric had kept an eye on you from the time you left Wethersham, knew you'd changed your name, even knew where you worked. It wasn't hard after that. I saw your photo on the Masters website and attended a few boring conferences before going to the right one and there you were – ripe for plucking.

'Do you know how difficult it's been pretending to be interested in your wittering for all these months. Putting up with your inane chat, your pathetic gratitude for my friendship. I was waiting for the right moment to destroy you, and it came. Your precious partnership, was the perfect time to strike.'

'You sent the emails?'

'Woohoo, give the girl a medal, she's copped on at last. Yes, you stupid cow, I sent the emails. They were the backup plan though.'

'Backup plan?' Melanie tried to clear a space in the fog. Oh God. *Hugo*. 'Hugo... you set that up?'

'It was a brilliant plan and would have worked but for two things: I hadn't taken Richard Masters' damn reasonableness into account and I never expected you to confess. You'd always spoken of him as a stiff, sanctimonious bastard. I assumed he'd chuck you on the scrapheap as soon as he discovered you'd messed up but no, of course not, you come out of it smelling of fucking roses.'

'Hardly.' It was all Melanie could think to say, her head reeling as she tried to come to terms with this new, shocking reality. 'You left the note here?'

Caitlin laughed. 'I was sorry I wasn't here to see your reaction. I bet it was priceless.'

'You picked the lock?'

'Even if I could do that, which I can't by the way, why would I? I have a key.' Caitlin laughed at Melanie's surprise. 'Remember when I went out to get food, and took your keys so I wouldn't disturb you? I had a copy made then.'

Melanie's head was throbbing, she held a hand up and rested it on her forehead before wiping away tears that were trickling down her cheeks. This was all too much. 'You were responsible for destroying Cherry too?' Expecting her to agree, Melanie blinked in confusion when Caitlin shook her head. 'I don't believe you.'

'There's no reason for me to lie anymore,' Caitlin said with a shrug. 'We divided the job, you see. I got you; Eric got Cherry.'

Feeling like a hornet's nest had exploded over her, Melanie shook her head, trying to clear her thoughts. 'No, now I know you're lying, he said he wasn't involved–'

'He wasn't, you fool,' Caitlin said coldly. 'Not in sending the emails to you. We had a good laugh about that when he told me. He sent the tweets about Cherry and painted some of the graffiti that appeared in the town. An added touch he was proud of.' Caitlin stopped and frowned. 'Surprisingly, he was upset at the outcome. He expected her to lose her job, but never expected her to take her own life. That's where we differed, you see, for me that was the perfect outcome.' Pushing away from the counter, she loomed over Melanie for a moment, smirking as she cringed, before pulling out a chair and sitting. 'It would have been so much easier if you'd followed suit, you know?'

Squeezing her eyes shut, Melanie gulped. 'It was you Eric warned me not to trust.'

'Did he really?' Caitlin seemed surprised.

'Yes, he wrote to me, told me to be careful who I trusted. I thought he was referring to Quinn.'

Caitlin's peal of laughter rang around the room, a sound that carried with it something nasty and foul and sent a shiver down Melanie's back. She looked at this woman she had called a friend and wondered how she'd been so badly fooled.

'That was so funny,' Caitlin said. 'You obviously fancied the guy so it was the icing on the cake to make you suspect him. And it hardly needed any prompting on my part, you were so confused after Hugo it was easy to make you second guess yourself.'

'You lied to me?'

'Of course I lied, you silly bitch.'

'But he took a key from my desk!' Or had he? Melanie had rummaged in her desk drawer, desperate to find evidence that Quinn was behind everything and had seen the missing key as proof. It was probably still there, wedged in a corner of the drawer. It was hard to believe that she'd been so wrong, that Caitlin was to blame for everything.

'I don't know what you're talking about,' Caitlin said, frowning.

Melanie shook her head. 'I made a mistake, forget it. You lied about Quinn being from Leeds?' It didn't matter, she just needed to keep Caitlin talking. The clock on the wall was ticking towards seven, any moment now, the doorbell would ring, announcing the estate agent's arrival. She had to be ready to scream for help.

'He's from Sussex if I remember rightly.' Caitlin laughed. 'You should have heard your gasp when I mentioned Leeds, it was really so funny.'

'You're mad,' Melanie said quietly, seeing the fanatical light in the woman's eyes. How had she never seen it before; how could Caitlin have disguised it for so long?

'Perhaps,' Caitlin said with a dismissive shrug.

'Are you going to tell me why? I assume you knew Matthew Thomas.'

Caitlin's expression changed, becoming twisted and ugly. 'Yes, I knew him.' She stood suddenly, pulling a knife from the magnetic holder. 'Not as big as I'd like but I suppose I can make do.' She sat back and folded her arms, the knife tucked into the crook of her elbow. 'Let me tell you a story,' she said in a sing-song voice. 'A long time ago, when I was sixteen, I attacked a classmate with a knife. He didn't die but my parents and the teachers, they said I wasn't...' She pulled one hand out, lifted her index finger and crooked it twice, '... quite right.' A smile hovered. 'I was lucky, it was an exclusive private school and they didn't want police involved. Instead, I spent a month in a psychiatric unit outside Manchester, and that's where I met Matthew.'

Caitlin's tone of voice changed from a dull monotone to

high-pitched excitement. 'I'd been there a week when he arrived. He was the most beautiful boy I'd ever seen and I was instantly and completely smitten. There were older girls who flirted with him but he wasn't very communicative with them, he seemed to prefer my more childlike attention and spent most of his time there with me.' Her voice trailed away and her eyes lost focus, drifting to the past, her face softening with the memories. 'Within a few days, we'd become lovers.'

Caitlin unfolded her arms and tapped the knife against the palm of her hand, the *slap-slap* a regular beat that didn't change as the sharp blade drew a fine red line across her palm; it didn't stop as tiny beads of blood went flying from the knife with each subsequent tap. 'I told him I'd find him when I was free, and the day after I left the clinic I hopped on a train and a bus and finally hitched a lift to Wethersham.' She looked at Melanie with hate-filled eyes. 'But when I found him, he didn't want to know.' The slap-slapping stopped, the silence filled with expectation. 'I was devastated and couldn't understand what I'd done so wrong, why he'd changed. But he wouldn't explain.' She looked at the knife, at the blood that was smeared across her palm and spattered across the table.

'Several months ago, we were investigating a gang who were exporting stolen cars and I called to Edgware Motors to speak to the manager there. I didn't recognise Eric, but obviously I haven't changed much over the years because he recognised me straight away.' Caitlin shrugged. 'He seemed to want to talk so I met him for a drink in the pub oppo–'

'The Londoner,' Melanie interrupted, grasping onto something in this conversation that she was sure of.

Tapping the blade of the knife against her hand, Caitlin shook her head. 'After all the years, Eric still hated you and that teacher, what's her name–'

'Cherry.' Melanie swallowed the dart of anger.

'Cherry, yes, her.' Caitlin drew a heavy breath. 'It wasn't until Eric explained what the two of you had done that I realised what... or should I say who... had changed my beautiful boy, and a red wave of anger and hatred for you both almost consumed me. It was you, Anne Edwards. You and your stupid fucking whispers that destroyed him.'

The knife tapping started again. Melanie watched blood spatter the table and tried to find the right words. 'I never meant things to go that far... I tried to stop it.' A psychiatric unit? Matthew had mental health problems. How could she have known he was so fragile, so vulnerable? No wonder her malicious lies had pushed him over the edge. If only she'd known... she liked to think she'd have been kinder, wouldn't have done what she'd done. Hindsight, it was such a slippery road.

'Nobody knew he had mental health issues,' she said. 'Maybe if we had–'

'Now, wouldn't that make it so much easier for you,' Caitlin interrupted her. 'Wouldn't that lift the burden of guilt from your pathetic shoulders. But I'm going to have to burst that particular comfy bubble, my dear friend. Matthew wasn't a patient, you fool, he was a volunteer. There was a group from a local school who came in to help the sickos like me to connect to the outside world. That's where Eric knew me from, he volunteered too. They moved to Wethersham a week before I was discharged. No, there's no help for you there, my dear, dear friend.'

She pointed the knife at Melanie. 'You changed my beautiful boy, you and your stupid whispers.'

30

Melanie's eyes were fixed on the knife as Caitlin spoke. All the years she'd struggled, was this the way it was going to end?

'It was your promotion to partner and Cherry's to school principal that sparked Eric's desire for revenge after all these years,' Caitlin said. 'I sat in that pub for an hour listening to him moan about how unfair it was that you were both so successful while poor Matthew never had the chance. He was obviously envious, drinking pints with whisky chasers and feeling sorry for himself. It wasn't hard to get him around to the idea of revenge.'

'It was your idea!'

Caitlin waved the knife. 'Let's say I encouraged his thinking. He was so drunk at that stage he was happy to agree to anything. It was definitely my idea to split the work. His role was to destroy Cherry and mine was to destroy you.' She pointed the knife at Melanie and grinned.

'That fool, Eric, hadn't realised he'd done such a good job until you told him Cherry had killed herself. I thought it was perfect, he was horrified and wanted to call a halt to it all.'

Melanie remembered the detective, Burke, saying that a woman could easily stab a man. 'You killed Eric.' It wasn't a question; Melanie knew suddenly with absolute conviction that she had.

'The fool was becoming a nuisance,' Caitlin said. 'Would you believe it, he said that Matthew's death had been avenged by Cherry's, that we'd done enough.' She uncrossed her arms and sliced the air with the knife. 'Enough talking.' She pulled a packet of pills from her pocket. 'You should have done a Cherry on it, of course, and taken your own life. That would have been the perfect outcome. But never mind, you can swallow these. You've been sounding more and more paranoid, nobody will be surprised when they find you.' Her smile chilled Melanie's blood. 'Not that it matters much anymore if it doesn't look like suicide. There are things happening that you don't know about so if you won't take them, I'll happily kill you slowly and very, very painfully.'

Melanie looked at the packet. Temazepam. She wondered how many it would take to kill her. She watched as Caitlin slid the foils from the packet and pressed the tablets out onto the table. There was no real reason to count, but Melanie did anyway. Twenty-eight tablets. She guessed that was more than enough to do the job.

'I'll take them,' she said, drawing cold eyes to her. 'I'm not good with pain, I'll take the damn tablets. But first, tell me, why?'

There was tense silence as Caitlin stared at her. 'Because, Anne Edwards, my whole fucking life is falling apart and it's all your fault. Or perhaps I should blame Hugo, but he's not here and you are.' Her laugh rang out again, making Melanie cringe. 'Of course, you don't know that part of the story either, do you? Hugo and I were old mates. He paid me well for information over the years and when I told him about my new friendship with you, you should have seen his eyes light up. I passed him the odd nugget of information that you dropped in conversation – did you never stop to ask why I was so interested in hearing about your boring job? God, you were so easy! Then, there was that merger. That really caught his fancy.'

'He was working for you.' Melanie wondered if her heart could really break.

Caitlin laughed, the sound sneering and nasty. 'Seriously, did you really think someone like Hugo would be interested in the likes of you?'

Melanie hadn't, she'd hoped, and for a moment, she'd believed. It was hard trying to understand that everything had been a lie. She remembered seeing Caitlin's reflection in the window. She thought she'd imagined the sneer; how could she have ever understood that was her real face? A horrific thought hit her. 'You killed him, didn't you?'

Caitlin shrugged dismissively. 'I'd only met him once, years ago. After that we communicated by phone. He didn't know who I was and it would have stayed like that.' She slammed her hand on the table, making Melanie jump and give a squeal of fright. 'Your fault again... everything your fault, Anne Edwards. Hugo insisted he needed more information than I could provide and worked out the plan to seduce you.' She sneered. 'Not that it took much, you were as he so elegantly put it *gagging for it* from day one.

'But then he saw that damn photograph you have in the living room and rang me, addressing me by my rank and name. The plan had been for him to cash in the shares when the price rose and disappear. But the damn shares didn't rise, they fell when the merger was delayed.

'He wasn't happy but neither was I. I didn't know the idiot had put his damn photo on that fake website. And thanks to you giving it to the police, I knew it wouldn't have been long before they identified him and brought him in. He'd have rushed to trade information for a lighter sentence and would have been delighted to have told them that DI Ballantyne was taking back-handers.'

Melanie tried to stay calm. Who was this monster she'd called a friend? Her eyes flicked to the clock. Five past seven. Wasn't it bloody typical of the agent to be late? Maybe, her heart sank, he wasn't going to come at all. She was fit and strong and she supposed there'd be an adrenaline rush if she was fighting for her life but she couldn't compete with the knife. The blade might not be long but it was obviously sharp.

When her eyes went back to the clock, Caitlin looked at her with a suspicious frown. 'Why do you keep looking at the time?'

Melanie didn't have to answer because the doorbell rang. She should have screamed, but stupidly she hesitated long enough to give Caitlin enough time to slap a hand over her mouth, pressing so hard Melanie felt her teeth bruise her gums. She would have tried to squirm free but she felt the chill of the knife blade scrape her neck.

'Not a word, not even a whimper or I'll slit your throat,' Caitlin snapped. 'Okay, who is it?' Removing her hand, she kept the knife pressed to her throat. 'Answer me.'

Melanie swallowed, trying to lubricate a suddenly dust-dry throat. 'It's an estate agent. I'm putting the apartment on the market. I arranged for him to call at seven.'

Caitlin growled as the doorbell chimed once more. 'He'll go away if it's not answered.'

'I told him I wanted it sold as soon as possible. I stressed the urgency of it. He might get suspicious if I don't answer. He might even worry that I've harmed myself and call the police.'

'Yes, like they're going to rush out because a doorbell isn't answered,' Caitlin said with heavy sarcasm but there was a hint of doubt in her eyes. When the doorbell sounded yet again moments later, she nudged Melanie's arm none too gently. 'Okay, put the chain on the door, then open it and tell him you've changed your mind. I'll be right behind you. If I hear the merest whisper of anything untoward, I'll drag him in and kill him, do you understand? Or do you want to be responsible for another man's death?'

'I understand.'

'Good, now get up.' The knife was moved from Melanie's neck to her back. She could feel the point of it stabbing through her shirt, a stinging sensation that said it had also pierced skin.

She moved jerkily, feeling a trickle of blood run down her back as the knife pressed harder. The doorbell rang again. He was being surprisingly persistent; she must have made her case more strongly that she'd thought or maybe it was that he really needed the commission. Her fingers fumbled with the safety chain, sliding it into place.

'Remember, I'm listening to every word,' Caitlin whispered, the knife pressing home her meaning.

Biting back a gasp of pain, Melanie nodded and pulled the door open, the safety chain halting movement within a couple of inches. 'Hi,' she said, the sound coming out as a pathetic squeak. She coughed to clear her throat and tried again. 'Hi,' she said more firmly. 'Listen, I'm really sorry but I've changed my mind.' Through the narrow gap, she could just about see him. He didn't seem too surprised despite his determined bell-ringing.

'Fine,' he said, reaching to hand her his card. 'If you change your mind, give me a shout, okay?'

It seemed the easiest thing to do, to take the damn card and send him safely on his way. 'Thank you, I'll certainly contact you if I change my mind and sorry again for dragging you he–' The door banging shut cut off her words, almost catching fingers that pulled back in time, the agent's card clutched between them. Feeling the press of the knife, she said nothing. They waited for a few seconds until they heard the distinct sound of receding footsteps.

'Right, inside,' Caitlin said.

In the kitchen, Melanie was pushed roughly into a chair. 'Don't move.' Caitlin grabbed a glass from the counter and turned on the tap.

Melanie would have tried to run but with the safety chain on the front door, that exit was closed to her. She'd be caught before she managed to open the door and Caitlin had already shown she wasn't averse to using the knife. Melanie turned the agent's card over in her fingers, jumping when a glass was slammed onto the table in front of her.

'It's time,' Caitlin said. 'I'm getting bored now.'

Melanie gulped. 'I need to use the loo.' When her request was met by an arched eyebrow, she looked down at the card in her hand. 'If I'm going to die, at least let me die with some dignity. I need to wee, if I don't go now... well, you know what will happen. I don't want my body lying in waste until it's found.'

Ignoring her, Caitlin gathered the pills into a neat pile. 'They're small, there won't be any problem in swallowing them.'

Her voice was kindly, reassuring even. It made Melanie shiver. 'Please,' she said, stretching a hand pleadingly across the table towards her, 'I really need '

'Shut up,' Caitlin snarled, her hand slapping the table so hard that the pills jumped and spread out. With a grunt, she gathered them together again with both hands and pushed them across the table. Melanie's hand was still stretched towards her, Caitlin sat back and looked at it as if considering the request.

When she picked up the knife, Melanie thought she was going to say yes, and use it as before to ensure her compliance as she went to the bathroom. Nothing could have prepared her for the suddenness of what happened next. In one smooth motion, and without the slightest change in her expression, Caitlin lunged with the knife and drove the point deep into the open beseeching palm, impaling Melanie's hand on the wood of the table beneath.

For the briefest of moments, the shock of the act numbed her. Dragging her eyes from Caitlin's fixed expression of disinterest, Melanie looked down to where blood was pooling in the palm of her hand. Searing pain shot from the wound and darted up her arm. She cried out, a scream of pain, terror and hopelessness as she stared at the hand that still clasped the knife handle. Caitlin was looking at her with a slight smile as if she were amused at Melanie's predicament. The smile turned mean and Melanie felt her gut clench as the knife moved. She thought it was going to be pulled out and braced herself for that but instead, it was twisted, first one way, then the other. Melanie screamed again, the agony unbearable.

Only then did Caitlin remove the knife.

Melanie dropped the card she'd been holding, grabbed her injured hand and watched as blood oozed out from between her fingers to drip onto her lap.

'Now you know what real pain is like,' Caitlin said, standing up and using the knife to indicate that Melanie follow suit. 'You can use the bathroom but keep that memory in the front of your mind. There'll be lots more if you try anything stupid.'

Melanie wasn't sure she could stand. The pain... she'd never felt anything like it. But she had to get up. It was her only chance. Staggering to her feet, she swayed a little, feeling weak and dizzy. She pressed her injured hand, the pain intensifying and focusing her, anger giving her strength. Leaving a trail of blood as she walked and ignoring the knife pressed to her back, she made it across the room into the hallway. The pain in her hand was intense. At the doorway of the bathroom, she reached out with her bloodstained uninjured hand and grasped the door frame.

'Get a move on,' Caitlin said.

Melanie pushed away and grasped the edge of the door. Inside, her attempt to shut it was stopped by the knife jabbing the wood inches from her fingers.

'Seriously,' Caitlin said, pulling the knife out and waving it in front of Melanie. 'You think I'm going to let you shut yourself in there and put me to the trouble of having to break the door down. Do you really want that?'

'I can't go with you looking at me. Please, close it over a little.' Melanie's voice was pleading, ending in a sob.

'You're such a pathetic, stupid cow.' Caitlin pulled the door towards her a little. 'Hurry up and have your piss, I'm getting bored.'

It was now or never. Taking Caitlin by surprise, Melanie shoved the door shut with all her remaining strength, ignoring the pain in her hand as her blood-slippery fingers fumbled with the lock, desperately trying to twist it as she heard a howl of anger from the other side and the door tremble as Caitlin threw herself against it. The click that told her the lock was engaged was almost lost in the screams of outrage.

'I'm going to cut you to pieces when I drag you out of there!'

Melanie sat on the edge of the bath, her eyes glued to the door as it was bombarded from the other side, the door shuddering with each blow. It wouldn't hold much longer, they weren't designed to protect against such rage, such ferocity. But she needed another minute. A savage yell preceded the next stronger blow and to her horror she saw the wood around the lock splinter. She climbed into the bath, no logic in the move, just sheer desperation, the pain in her hand vanishing in the all-consuming terror that one more determined push by Caitlin would send the door flying open.

And then, she thought she heard something else. Further away... a loud crash... raised voices followed by screams and shouts, the smashing of furniture and crashing of glass. Melanie reached for a towel from the rail and wrapped it around her bleeding, throbbing hand as the sounds of chaos continued to rock the apartment. Her vision blurred, but she fought to stay conscious. She'd come through so much, she wasn't leaving the fight until she was sure it was all over.

'Melanie?' A voice she hadn't expected to hear. 'Melanie, are you okay, can you open the door?'

The pain in her hand was agonising. She couldn't move, she couldn't even answer the increasingly desperate calling of her name. She'd been so wrong about so much, even about the man on the other side of the door.

A loud crack and the bathroom door flew open. Liam Quinn, looking dishevelled, rushed through, stopping when he saw her.

'Melanie!'

DI Elliot pushed past him and crouched down beside the bath. 'Where are you hurt?'

'Just my hand,' Melanie said, lifting it up to show him. 'And there is a cut on my back. That's all.' And that was all. She was alive. 'You have her?'

'Yes, they're taking her away. She won't cause you any more problems.'

'She killed Hugo,' Melanie said, tears catching in her throat. 'And Eric.'

The sound of a siren grew louder. 'Don't worry about all of that now,' Elliot said. 'She'll pay for what she did.'

'You don't understand,' Melanie said. 'It's all my fault.'

Before she had a chance to explain, paramedics arrived.

They ignored her insistence that she could walk and lifted her gently onto a gurney to wheel into the ambulance. Her hand was bandaged and she was given something for the pain. She didn't know what it was, but she was out of it all before the ambulance left Bloom Park Road.

31

The first thing Melanie realised when she woke was that the pain had gone. It was such a relief that she lay without opening her eyes, enjoying the sensation, unwilling to rejoin the human race to enter a different world of agony. *Caitlin.* How could she cope with that? Silent tears squeezed out from the corners of Melanie's eyes and ran down the side of her face into her hair. For a fleeting moment, she wished she'd taken the pills and would not have to cope with everything, the endless prying questions, the revelations about her past. Because it would all come out now.

'Hey, don't cry.'

Startled, her eyes snapped open and she turned her head to look straight into a pair of bloodshot grey eyes. 'Quinn,' she said, in a barely audible whisper.

His forehead creased. 'Should I call the nurse, are you in pain?'

Melanie lifted her hand. It was swathed in bandages, looking for all the world like a bright-white boxing glove. She'd obviously been out for a considerable amount of time. Her eyes flicked around. A cubicle. Hospital. Probably A and E. Her brain was processing the information in bite-sized portions. 'No,' she said, and shut her eyes again, allowing the tears to continue. She couldn't have stopped them if she tried.

She heard Quinn move and felt herself being lifted forward and enfolded into his strong, capable arms. It would have been nice to have lain there and given way to it. But the double betrayal of Hugo and Caitlin bit deep, it would be a long time before she would be able to trust again, to depend on anyone again. 'I'm okay,' she said, pushing him away. Staying sitting up, she ran her hand through her tangled hair and stared at him. 'How long have I been here?'

'About six hours. A doctor saw you shortly after we brought you in and he had your hand x-rayed. There's no damage to bone or ligaments, just some soft tissue injury. He put in a few stitches and said it should heal without problem.' Quinn sat back in his chair with a heavy sigh. 'She fooled everyone, Melanie.'

He didn't understand, how could he when he didn't know all the story. 'Did the doctor say when I could go home?'

It looked as if Quinn wanted to say more but instead, he shook his head. 'He said there was no need to admit you so you can go whenever you want. You can, he said, return to outpatients to have the dressing changed or attend your local GP.' Quinn reached into his pocket. 'He gave me a prescription for painkillers. He said you'd probably need some.'

She shook her head. 'The pain seems to have eased.' A slight ache had returned but nothing like the agony she remembered.

Quinn smiled. 'They gave you an injection when you were admitted. It'll start to wear off soon so we'd better get this filled before we leave.'

We. Caitlin had lied about him, true. But what did Melanie really know about him? Swinging her feet to the floor, she ignored his outstretched hand and stood up. 'If you give it to me,

I can sort that myself and get a taxi to take me home. You don't owe me anything, Mr Quinn.'

'I'm afraid you can't go home yet.'

She felt the first stirring of anger. 'Really?'

He held his hands up. 'Sam Elliot. He's been in and out a few times. He's anxious to get a statement from you. I told him I'd stay and let him know as soon as you were awake enough to speak to him.' Quinn looked at her with a sardonic smile. 'I guess that time has come.'

Her shoulders slumped. Before, when she couldn't cope, she'd call Caitlin for support. 'Not now,' she said, hating how pathetic she sounded. 'Please, I couldn't bear to talk about it now.'

Quinn pulled out his mobile. 'Sam, it's Liam. I'm taking her home. She's happy to make a statement in the morning, okay? She's concerned that with the morphine she's had, she won't be able to remember all the details.' He listened for a moment and held the phone away from his mouth to address her. 'Sam says he'll call around first thing unless you want to go into the station?'

Melanie didn't even try to hide her gratitude. 'No, thank you, ask him to call around.' There was no room for anger anymore; Quinn wasn't to blame for the state her life was in. She was good at messing up, she always had been.

It was easier to allow him to sort everything out. She leaned on his arm as they made their way from the hospital and sat in his car as he had the prescription filled, resting her head back, trying to fight tears that were never far away. She didn't speak when he pulled up outside a house she didn't recognise, merely looking at him with a raised eyebrow.

'It's my home,' he said, 'the crime-scene people are finished with your place but Sam says it's in a bit of a mess. I have a spare room you can use until it's sorted. He'll call here in the morning. We'd discussed it while you were still out.'

Discussed it and made decisions for her. Lethargy swept over her, swamping the residual terror, the deep-seated hurt and betrayal. She said nothing as she climbed from the car and walked beside him to the front door. He was speaking but she didn't hear what he was saying, shutting herself off, following where he led, where he directed until finally, she shut the spare bedroom door.

He'd kindly given her a T-shirt to wear. The hospital staff had cut the sleeve of her bloodstained shirt. Along the seam, she noticed, as if in the future she'd think of sewing it up to wear again. With a tug, she managed to tear it further and eased her bandaged hand out. Blood had oozed through to her bra, she looked at the dark-red stains, then hurriedly unhooked it and threw it on top of her discarded shirt.

It would have been nice to have had a shower, to wash away the faint traces of blood she could see on her skin but she was weak, exhausted, diminished by all that had happened so that she thought she might fade away, slip down the plughole and vanish. Or was that a case of wishful thinking?

A gentle knock on the door made her scurry to pull the T-shirt over her head, her bandaged hand easily slipping through the armhole. If she were worried about being decent, she needn't have done, it hung down to her knees. 'Yes,' she said, watching as the door opened slowly.

Quinn held out a glass of water and a packet of tablets. 'You should probably take them before you go to sleep.'

The ache in her hand had become a dull throb. It would probably get worse. She held out her hand for the packet, shaking her head when he offered to open it. 'I can manage,' she said, and proved her point by opening it and removing two pills.

Throwing them into her mouth, she reached for the glass of water and took a gulp.

'If you need anything during the night... or what's left of it,' he added with a slight smile, 'yell, my room is next door.'

She couldn't shake off the lethargy to find the words to reply, to thank him for being with her, for looking out for her. Maybe there were no words. Without waiting for him to leave the room, she pulled back the duvet and climbed into bed.

The painkillers must have been strong. Within a very short time, the pain had eased and she slipped into a deep sleep.

It wasn't pain or even the light that shone through the open curtains that woke her. It was the sense of despair that made her completely alert within seconds, the events of the previous day cascading around her, all of it so unbelievable that if it weren't for the discomfort in her hand, she'd have thought that maybe it had been a dream, or a nightmare. She'd no idea of the time or how long she'd been asleep. The house was quiet. Perhaps she was alone.

Her mouth was dry and her head thumping. She needed a drink. Throwing back the duvet, she sat on the edge of the bed until her head stopped swimming. The painkillers sat on the bedside table, she guessed they'd been responsible for her deep sleep. Her hand ached but she had a vague idea that she'd agreed to DI Elliot coming around to take a statement and wanted to have her wits about her. After everything she'd been through, she could handle an ache.

The T-shirt she wore was heavy cotton and far preferable to wear than the bloodstained clothes that were strewn on the floor. She opened the bedroom door and listened, her head tilting slightly as she heard the faint murmur of voices. Edging down the stairway, she stopped when the voices were a little clearer but she was still unable to hear what they said or identify the voices. Both were male, it was a fair bet it was Quinn and Elliot.

There being no point lurking on the stairs, she took the last few steps down to the hallway. Old, probably original Victorian tiles covered the floor. They were cold under her bare feet, reminding her of that terrifying moment when she'd stepped into the bath. Caitlin's murderous screams seemed to echo in her ears and it was a few minutes before Melanie had the strength to move.

An ornate coat stand stood inside the front door. She recognised Elliot's rather tatty brown raincoat. The only other garment hanging from it was a brown man's jacket. No female's coat, no children's clutter. It looked as if Quinn might live alone.

The voices were coming from a room at the end of the hall. She hesitated outside, then with the bravery that comes with having known terror, she grabbed hold of the handle and pushed the door open. She held onto it as conversation died and the two men turned and jumped to their feet. 'Hi.' It was all she could manage.

The room wasn't large and it was cluttered, every surface covered with paraphernalia. The kitchen, which had probably started its life as a galley-kitchen, lay along one wall. Most of the rest of the room was occupied by the overlarge table where the men had been seated.

'Sit down,' Quinn said, pulling out a chair. 'I'll make fresh coffee.'

'Thank you, coffee is just what I need.' Melanie slid onto the chair, pulling the T-shirt down over her knees. Looking up, she caught DI Elliot's sympathetic gaze and gave him a slight smile.

'How's the hand?'

She lifted her bandaged hand and twisted it back and

forward. 'It's okay,' she said, ignoring the twinge as she rested it on the table in front of her. 'I can't complain, I'm here to tell you my tale, there was a time yesterday when I didn't think I would be.'

Elliot's face was sombre as he jerked his head towards Quinn. 'You can thank Liam.'

Raising her eyebrow in surprise, she looked over to where he was filling a cafetière. 'It sounds like we all have a tale to tell.' She waited until coffee was in front of her, took a sip and sighed. 'Right,' she said firmly. 'You first.'

Elliot smiled. 'Simple, really. After I left you in the pub, I headed back to the station. To my surprise, Liam was waiting for me.'

'I was worried.' Quinn took over the story. 'Someone was telling you lies about me so you wouldn't trust me. Now why would someone do that? I decided it was worth speaking to Sam to see if he knew what was going on. Luckily for me,' he said, throwing her a sharp glance, 'I had a strong alibi for the morning Eric Thomas was killed.'

She looked from one to the other. 'I still don't understand; how did you know it was Caitlin?'

Quinn smiled. 'I remembered you'd said, *Thanks to Caitlin*, you knew all about me. When I told Sam that…'

'What you didn't know, Melanie,' Elliot explained, 'is that DI Ballantyne has been the focus of an investigation by police standards and the IOPC. The Independent Office for Police Conduct,' he clarified, seeing Melanie's blank look. 'I don't know all the details but suffice to say they were closing in on her. When Liam said Caitlin had told you about him, I checked, and as you know, everything she'd told you was a lie.'

'She fooled me completely.' Melanie's voice was heavy with despair and a crippling sadness.

Elliot frowned. 'She fooled a lot of people.' His expression was grim. 'If you hadn't told me about Wethersham and those emails, I probably wouldn't have been able to put it together. She'd lied about Liam, it had to be for a good reason and it rang a warning bell. The investigating officer on Eric's murder kept me in the loop so I found out that he'd been killed in the same way as Hugo, a single lethal stab wound. We had a long conversation, both of us did some digging, and quickly found out that the only thing the two men had in common... the only common denominator... was you.' He gave a quick smile. 'I didn't see you as a murderer, but Ballantyne had lied for a reason and through you, she was also connected to both men. It was tenuous' – he shook his head – 'but something felt wrong about it all.'

Melanie sipped her coffee pensively. 'How did you know she was in my apartment?'

'I decided to have a chat with her and contacted her office. Nobody had seen her so I rang her mobile. She made a mistake taking her work phone with her. When she didn't answer, I had them trace it. As soon as we realised where she was, when you weren't answering your mobile or landline, that warning bell sounded even louder.'

'She told me my landline was off the hook and fixed it, she was obviously taking it off,' Melanie said with a shake of her head. 'She threw my mobile across the room and it came apart.' Melanie met Quinn's eyes with a hint of apology. 'I was still blaming you, you know, but when she asked if you were responsible for the emails as well, she gave herself away. I'd never told her about them, you see.' She guessed by the knowledge in his eyes that Elliot had filled him in on her history. 'He told you?' she asked, jerking her head towards the detective. She waited for Quinn's nod before putting her coffee down. 'Good, it'll make my part of the story easier to tell.'

She told them as much as she could recall, from the moment Caitlin had arrived at her door to when they'd come bursting into the bathroom. 'Five months I've known her and I never suspected a thing.' She sat back and stared at her bandaged hand, remembering the knife that had been impaled in it so callously. 'What kind of an idiot does that make me? What does it say about my judgement?'

'She fooled a lot of people,' Elliot said. 'For goodness' sake, she made it to detective inspector without anyone being any the wiser. I gather from the IOPC that concerns were only raised a few months ago but their investigation has uncovered irregularities going back years.'

'She was very clever,' Quinn said.

'Luckily for me, so were you,' Melanie said, looking from one to the other. 'That was very clever, what you did.'

'We were down the street from your house trying to plan what to do when the estate agent turned up.' Elliot grinned. 'We couldn't believe our luck. When we explained the situation to him, he was more than happy to give us one of his business cards and leave it to us.'

'Then it was a case of trying to decide what to write,' Quinn said. 'It had to be something short and simple but a message you would understand and act on.'

Melanie remembered turning the card over and over between her fingers. It was a few seconds before she'd realised there was something written on the reverse. *Police. 5 minutes. Bathroom.* 'When I saw it first, in my confusion, I thought you were going to come through the bathroom in five minutes,' she said with a half-hearted smile. 'It was a few more seconds before I realised you wanted me to go in there.'

'We wanted you out of the way, desperation can drive people to do wicked things,' Elliot said. 'We were afraid, if we stormed the place, she would kill you before we could stop her. After all, we were pretty sure she'd already killed two people, so she'd nothing to lose.'

'That was why she stabbed me,' Melanie said. 'She wanted me to realise that she wouldn't hesitate to hurt me if I tried anything.'

'But you were still brave enough to move when you had the chance and to get that bathroom door shut.' Quinn's voice was full of admiration, his grey eyes warm. 'She'd almost got through the door when we arrived.'

'I saw the wood splinter and hoped you'd get there on time.'

There was an uneasy silence as all three considered how close it had been. Without a word, Quinn stood and moved back to the kitchen. Neither Elliot nor Melanie spoke while Quinn refilled the kettle, took bread from the fridge and made several slices of toast.

Minutes later, a plate of hot buttered toast was put in the middle of the table and fresh coffee poured into each mug.

Melanie thought she'd never tasted anything as good and licked the dripping butter from her fingers before reaching for a second slice.

'It was odd,' Elliot said, wiping toast crumbs from the front of his shirt. 'Once she realised she was caught, all the fight seemed to go out of her and she couldn't confess to everything she'd done fast enough.'

Melanie, about to take a bite from her second slice, froze with her mouth open and the toast suspended. 'She confessed?'

Nodding, he reached for his coffee, gulping some down before he continued. 'It was as if we'd lanced a boil, everything came spewing out, things we didn't know about, things I'm pretty sure the IOPC didn't know about.' He reached for another slice of toast, but before he took a bite, he added, 'She asked to see you, Melanie.'

32

Of course, Melanie had to go. She wanted to confront the monster, now she'd seen it without its mask.

'I'll need to call in home first,' she said, pulling at the fabric of the T-shirt. 'I'm not going to see her like this.'

'I'll make a few calls to arrange things,' Elliot said. 'We can drop by your place on the way.'

The silence following his departure was tense, heavy. Her eyes were fixed on her bandaged hand, her thoughts on what Caitlin might say. She raised her eyes to find Quinn regarding her with a slight smile.

'You know all about me now, don't you? About all the pain I caused,' she said quietly. She watched him nod and pressed her lips together. 'I was young–'

'You were a child,' he interrupted her. 'Merely a child, you didn't deserve to suffer so badly for doing childish things.'

Strangely, for all the hours she'd spent with counsellors, nobody had ever put it so simply. Inside, the tight coils relaxed, just a little. 'I'm not a child now and I was blaming you, accusing you–'

He held a hand up, stopping her. 'Caitlin Ballantyne fooled

everyone. You thought you could trust her because she'd spent the last few months making you believe you could. She used your past to manipulate you, then she lied to you.' Reaching out, he put a finger under Melanie's chin and lifted it. 'You might think it was all about you, and what happened when you were a child, but that doesn't account for the backhanders she took long before she met you, or for the way she used information she stole from you to make herself a tidy sum of money. She is a bad 'un, Melanie.'

It was still too hard to separate the friend she thought she'd known from the woman who would murder and cheat. So hard to understand... to believe... that the friendship was part of her manipulative plan to get revenge. She needed to know how much of what Caitlin had done was her fault. It was all very well for Quinn to tell her none of it was, but that niggling guilt, that desperate memory of those awful words she had whispered that had destroyed Matthew, they wouldn't go away. If Caitlin told her that his death had been responsible for the wrong path she'd taken, Melanie didn't think she'd be able to cope.

Elliot returned, pulling on his coat. 'We need to get moving. I've arranged for you to speak to her in an hour.'

Melanie looked at him, appalled. An hour? 'That doesn't give me much time. I really need to have a shower.'

'There's plenty of time,' he said, holding the door open. 'Less time for thinking and worrying too.'

On that count, he was right. Both men went into the apartment with her. She didn't have time to survey the damage. Someone, she noticed, had wiped away the drips of blood from the hall floor and the bathroom. She was relieved and ridiculously grateful not to see that evidence of her nightmare.

Leaving the two men in the living room, she chose what to wear and hurried into the bathroom. The door didn't lock, it barely shut. With her foot, she moved a rubbish bin in front of it.

That would have to suffice. It was awkward with her bandaged hand and impossible to scrub herself the way she desperately wanted to. The shower gel proved impossible to open with one hand, it slipped and landed with a bang on the shower tray. She kicked it to one side and picked up her shampoo. Easier to open, she squirted it all over and washed.

Conscious of the time constraints, she rinsed the suds off, switched off the shower and stepped out. It took longer than usual to dress, her hand proving to be not only cumbersome but awkward. The fine-knit jumper she'd chosen was loose-fitting but the material kept snagging on the dressing and it was also surprisingly difficult to do up the zip on her trousers with one hand. She towel-dried her hair. It would have been nice to have worn it in her customary chignon, but there was no point in attempting such impossibilities. Instead, she brushed it back and left it loose.

'Okay, I'm good to go,' she said, stepping into the living room.

Two sets of eyes swept over her, both assessing, one warmly admiring. 'You managed despite your hand,' Quinn said. 'You look much better.'

She smiled. She'd looked like death; anything would have been an improvement.

There was little conversation on the way to the police station. She sat in the passenger seat, her eyes fixed on the road as Elliot negotiated the traffic, taking roads she'd never been on before and getting them there, to her surprise, with ten minutes to spare.

Inside, she and Quinn followed him blindly down corridors and through doorways until finally they reached their destination. 'She's insisting that she sees you alone,' Elliot said, with a grim expression on his usually genial face. 'I don't know if you're happy with that?'

Melanie wasn't happy being there, full stop, but she needed

to be if she wasn't going to spend the rest of her life haunted by unanswered questions. 'I'm assuming she won't have a knife,' she said, with an attempt at humour that raised an eyebrow rather than a smile. 'No, I'll be fine,' she said, impatient to get on with it, to get it over with.

'We will be watching and listening.' He opened the door and pointed to the mirror on the wall. 'It's two-way.'

Like on the TV, she thought. Her life had turned into a damn TV programme. Apart from the mirror, the only furniture in the room was a table bolted to the floor, and two flimsy plastic chairs. She took the one on the far side of the table, the chair creaking as she sat.

'You'll be okay,' Quinn said, giving her a reassuring smile.

When the door shut after them, Melanie immediately wanted to call them back as fear slithered down her spine. She wished she'd sat in the other chair. Here, she was facing the mirror, they'd be able to see every nervous tic, every bead of sweat that pinged. Her mouth was suddenly dust dry. When the door opened, she felt her heart race but it wasn't Caitlin.

'I thought you might want some water,' Quinn said, putting a plastic beaker on the table in front of her.

Her lower lip trembled, her hand seeking the beaker, bringing it to her lips and taking a long gulp. 'Thank you,' she said, her voice choking.

'We're only through there,' he said, resting a hand on her shoulder. 'If we see anything amiss, we'll come straight in, okay?'

She took a deep breath and let it out in a sigh.

Her hand was beginning to ache. It served to remind her exactly what kind of a woman Caitlin was and strengthened her backbone when the door opened for the second time and two uniformed constables escorted Caitlin into the room.

Melanie thought she'd struggle with separating the friend she thought she'd had from the monster who'd wanted to kill her but when she looked across the table, she barely recognised the woman sitting there. Caitlin had always appeared so vital, she'd held herself with an almost military bearing, upright and poised. And there was a certain something that drew your eye to her. The woman who slouched opposite with dull eyes and a lax, loose-lipped mouth wasn't the woman she'd known.

Melanie dropped her eyes to her bandaged hand and bit her lip. But then, the woman she'd known hadn't existed.

There was silence broken only by Caitlin's heavy breathing.

Melanie wanted to sit it out; to not be the one who gave in and said the first word, but after ten minutes of silence she burst out, 'Why, Caitlin?'

A petty smile of satisfaction appeared, but it faded quickly and once more Caitlin looked dull and vacant. 'You know why, Anne Edwards.'

The words, an eerie similarity to an email Caitlin had sent her, made Melanie shiver. 'Because of Matthew Thomas,' she said, half-expecting the vicious reaction she got the last time she'd said his name but this time there was no response at all. When several minutes passed without another word, she stood up. 'I came because you asked for me, but I've no intention of waiting here while you decide to speak.'

'He was the only one I've ever really loved.'

Melanie sat on the edge of the chair, her shoulders drooping in sorrow as she remembered the boy they'd both admired. They had that in common. 'Matthew was very handsome.'

'We were supposed to be together.'

'I'm sorry,' Melanie said, words she had said so many times. Such pain she had caused with her stupid, twisted whispers. She'd destroyed Matthew's life, messed up her own, and now it seems she'd messed up Caitlin's too.

Melanie had made this monster.

'I didn't mean to cause such pain. If I'd known how fragile he was, that my stupid gossip would push him over the edge, I'd never–' She didn't finish, startled into silence by Caitlin's sudden laughter.

The laughter stopped as quickly as it had begun and Caitlin gave her a pitying look. 'Everything's about you, isn't it? But you know nothing. Matthew wasn't the least bit fragile, he was steaming angry when I met him. Angry and cruel... he told me to get lost, that he hadn't meant any of the words he'd said to me. That he'd just wanted to fuck me.' Caitlin's laughter was edged with mania. 'I believed him, I thought I'd been a fool. It wasn't until I spoke to Eric that I knew the truth but it was too late of course. Too late to change what had happened by the river.'

Melanie frowned. 'You were there when he jumped?'

Caitlin squeezed her eyes shut. When they opened, they were pitiless holes of horror. 'He didn't jump, Mel.'

An angry boy, a distraught, rejected young girl. The picture was easy to visualise. The riverbank was steep, it crumbled at the edges, and the river was fast-flowing. One push, Matthew wouldn't have had a chance. 'You pushed him?'

33

Hampered by handcuffs, Caitlin still managed to lunge part way across the table, her face twisted in anger. 'I'd gone to Wethersham to be with him... the way we'd planned and dreamed... but he told me to get lost, that he hadn't meant a word he'd said. You know what rejection is like, don't you, Melanie? That was why you started those damn rumours in the first place. Well, my revenge was more immediate.'

Caitlin flopped back on her chair and for a moment the only sound in the room was her heaving breath. When she spoke again, her voice was barely audible and Melanie was forced to lean closer to hear. She could smell the foetid breath that wafted from her in gusts as if it came from a part of her that was rotting... or maybe rotten. She sat back, she didn't want to hear any more.

But Caitlin wasn't finished. 'He turned away from me, picked up a handful of stones and started throwing them into the river... as if I wasn't there, as if the days and hours we'd spent together meant nothing. I watched the muscles in his back as he pulled his arm up to throw, and remembered running my hands down his naked skin... the warmth, the smell of him... and I begged...' Her voice cracked, her joined hands rising to wipe tears away. She snuffled noisily before going on with her story.

'I begged, but he ignored me, kept on throwing those fucking stones, each one hitting the water with a plop and disappearing.' Caitlin mimed throwing an imaginary stone, the cuffs jingling. 'I was crying so hard, tears and snot were running down my face. I wiped them away with the back of my hand, then stared at the gelatinous, disgusting slime trail, the evidence of my sorrow. Matthew still had his back to me and the broad expanse of his khaki green jacket was too tempting to resist.' She tilted her head, confused. 'I'd swear it was all I'd planned to do... simply wipe all traces of the mess away... but he vanished.' She shrugged. 'Poof! Just like that, without a sound.'

Melanie couldn't think of anything to say. She wasn't sure she could handle this truth.

'I made my way back home then and got on with my life. Thanks to the clinic and counsellors I learned how to handle my anger, or at least to hide it. And until I met Eric, I never knew the truth.' Caitlin's mouth twisted. 'All these years, rejection has been curdling in my brain. When I found out what you'd done, that it was thanks to your damn whispers that my beautiful boy had changed, I wanted to destroy you.'

They sat in silence for a moment. Melanie's eyes flickered to the mirror behind as she tried to make sense of Caitlin's warped logic. She wondered if the men observing had been as shocked as she at Caitlin's cold words. It was difficult to take it all in. Matthew hadn't committed suicide... Melanie wasn't to blame for his death. She felt the massive load that had weighed her down for so many years lift and float away. Caitlin was staring at her, waiting for her to comment. What was left to say? 'Why did you want to see me?'

'I wanted to destroy you, ruin your career and when that failed, to take your life but that plan also failed.' Caitlin lifted both her hands in a what-can-I-do gesture. 'It looks like I'm going away for a long time, it seemed unfair that I couldn't accomplish something of what I'd planned. That's why I decided to tell you the truth about what happened to Matthew.' Her smile held no trace of humour. 'All those years you felt guilty, I wanted you to know they were in vain, that you lost a lifetime for something you didn't do, that you wasted it all.' The smile faded, her face once again sunken and slack-jawed. 'It is some consolation to me.'

So many years... Melanie's eyes filled with tears. The feeling of guilt had lifted, not completely, the part she'd had in the drama that had unfolded all those years before was far smaller than she'd thought, but it had been enough to set a catastrophic series of events into play. And her dreadful whispers had echoed through the years to cause more deaths, more chaos.

And Caitlin was right too. On top of the senseless waste of life, Matthew, Eric, even Hugo, were the years she'd wasted on guilty self-flagellation. *You always made a mess of things.*

But then cutting across her mother's words came Quinn's clearer ones, *You were merely a child, you didn't deserve to suffer so badly for doing childish things.*

Maybe, at last, it was time to stop punishing herself. Melanie lifted her chin and stared across the table. 'No,' she said with a slow shake of her head. 'I didn't waste it all. I am still a corporate lawyer. Still a junior partner despite your attempts to ruin me.' She lifted her bandaged hand. 'This will heal. I hope it leaves a scar to remind me just what a piece of shit you really are.'

Using her good hand for leverage, she pushed to her feet. 'The future is mine. The future, Caitlin. I have one. You, however, don't.' She waved to the two-way mirror behind Caitlin's head. 'You tried to turn me against Liam Quinn but he is one of the good ones. Him, Sam Elliot, Dan, Richard Masters. So much good in my life, I wasn't able to see it clearly before but

I can now.' She looked down on her erstwhile friend. 'You failed again, Caitlin. And you've run out of chances.'

Outside, Liam Quinn was waiting for her. 'You did well,' he said.

Before paranoia and Caitlin's lies had swayed her, Melanie had thought of him as a brace for her backbone, as one of the good guys. His warm grey eyes held hers and she smiled. She'd been right, her mother had been wrong. She didn't always mess things up at all. She'd made one stupid mistake. It was time to stop paying for it.

The sun was shining as they exited the building. 'Do you know what I'd like now,' she said, turning to look at Quinn.

'A Lagavulin?'

She smiled and hooked her arm in his. 'No, I think this day calls for champagne.'

THE END

ACKNOWLEDGEMENTS

As ever, grateful thanks to all in Bloodhound Books, especially Betsy Reavley, Tara Lyons, Heather Fitt, Morgen Bailey and Ian Skewis.

When you work so hard on a story you want people to read it – so a huge thanks to all who read, to the bloggers who get the word out and everyone who leaves a review – always such a relief to see when people enjoy what you wrote.

The support from the writing community is fantastic and an author's world would be a lonelier place without it – so a special thanks to the writers Jenny O'Brien, Leslie Bratspis, Pat Gitt, Mary Karpin, Pam Lecky, Vikki Patis, Michael Scanlon and Jim Ody for your continued support and encouragement.

A huge thank you also to the wonderful support from the following Facebook groups and their administrators: Caroline Maston, David Gilchrist and Samantha Brownley of the UK Crime Book Club; Andi Miller of Skye's Mum and Books; Dee Groocock of Book on the Positive Side; Susan Hunter and Anita Waller of Crime Fiction Addict; and Keri Beevis, Patricia Dixon, Heather Fitt and Anita Waller of The Paperback Writers.

Thanks to my husband, Robert, my sisters, brothers, extended family and my friends for always being there.

On a technical side, thanks to Alan Wallace, Administrative Officer, Royal Parks Dept for information regarding mobile phone coverage in Richmond Park, and to Roz in the Freedom of Information Triage Team, Metropolitan Police Service.

I love to hear from readers and can be contacted here:

www.facebook.com/valeriekeoghnovels
Twitter: @ValerieKeogh1
Instagram: valeriekeogh2

Printed in the USA
CPSIA information can be obtained
at www.ICGtesting.com
LVHW090810131023
760664LV00008B/640